Seventeen-year-old Alisha

She's had to rescue her headstrong little brother from getting eaten by an extradimensional monster, her mom has put her on dish duty as punishment for bringing her sword to the table (again), and her lifelong enemy, snarky rich girl Belladonna, is starting to look like both a real human being and someone Alisha would like to kiss.

Oh, and to make matters worse, it looks like the world is about to end.

GUARDIANS

T.J. Baer

A NineStar Press Publication
www.ninestarpress.com

Guardians

First Edition, July 2023

ISBN: 978-1-64890-678-7

Also available in eBook, ISBN: 978-1-64890-677-0

CONTENT WARNING:

This book contains depictions of the death of a minor character.

For my grandmother, Donna Williams, who started the magic.

Chapter One

My brother Jake lay unconscious on the cave floor, his favorite denim jacket torn in three places and his cell phone a cracked mess of plastic on the ground. If we actually survived this, he was going to be pissed.

"All right, look," I said, giving the giant snarling insect monster my serious face. "I know I don't look like much, but you should know I am fully capable of kicking your big buggy butt straight back to where it came from, not only for hurting my brother, but for whatever unholy reign of terror you've got planned here."

The monster was nine feet tall, jet-black, and scaly, with hundreds of spindly legs, like a centipede on steroids. Savage mandibles gleamed in the light from the cave mouth, and I tightened my grip on my sword hilt. And because times of stress often led me to incredible feats of word vomit, I kept talking.

"I mean, let's face it: guys like you don't generally show up in our world without some kind of nasty plan for world domination, so I think it's pretty safe to say you're up to no good. So are you gonna go peacefully, or do I have to start shoving my boot up random orifices until we find the one that hurts the most?"

The centipede monster reared back, its legs fanning out, its mandibles opening—

And then it tilted its scaly head to the side as if regarding me in puzzlement. "You speak great volumes but say very little," it said in a thin, whistling voice.

Which, okay, was fair. I'd always had a tendency to babble, particularly when I was in imminent danger of being devoured by the Godzilla of centipedes. Generally, the centipede didn't take the time to inform me of it though.

"I do not wish any harm upon you," it continued, deviating even further from the Evil Monster Intent on Taking Over the Earth speech. "Nor any human. I came here only wishing to be left alone, but your companion—" It swung its head toward Jake. "—attempted to steal one of my children, at which point I was forced to defend them. I have not seriously harmed him, only caused him to lose consciousness to neutralize him as a threat."

"He tried to steal one of your *kids?*" That didn't sound like Jake.

The centipede-thing tilted its head toward the other end of the cave, where I could just make out the glittering of a number of round, pearly, head-sized spheres. Eggs? They looked like the kind of pretty, decorative objects people would pay a lot of money for, bringing them much more firmly into the realm of things Jake would totally try to steal.

I sighed and slid my sword into its sheath. The magic triggered the instant I did, and sword and sheath shrank to being a decorative golden clasp on my belt. "I apologize for my companion's rash actions," I said, bowing my head slightly like we were supposed to do in these situations. "If you'd allow me to remove him from here, I swear to you that he'll never come near you or your children again."

The centipede bowed its head too, its pincers snapping and clicking together in a way that I tried not to be too creeped out by. "That would be acceptable. I thank you, Guardian."

I blinked. "How'd you know I'm a Guardian?"

"Well, for one thing, the sword."

"Ah."

"But even had you come unarmed, I would have known. You wear your status like a cloak. It seeps from every ounce of your being, every word and action. Though you look a frail female thing, there is power in you."

"Frail female thing," I said in a flat voice and decided not to be offended. If the worst thing a giant centipede monster had to throw at me was sexism, I could probably count myself lucky. "Yeah, well, guess I'd better get Jake—err, my companion—out of your hair before he wakes up and starts trying to make off with your kids again."

I started forward, hoping the centipede monster would move out of the way, but it stayed where it was, its black eyes glittering in the dimness.

"You have shown me respect and kindness, and so I shall do something for you in return. My species have a unique ability that appears only between laying our eggs and the birth of our children."

"Oh, yeah? What kind of ability?"

"The ability to glimpse the future. It allows us to provide extra protection to our young when they are unable to protect themselves, for instance if a young human is attempting to steal one of them."

"For instance," I said dryly.

"Something lurks on the horizon, Guardian. An age of darkness and danger is coming to you and those like you."

I frowned. "To the Guardians, you mean?"

"To all beings of your world."

"What kind of danger?"

Its legs rippled, and it dropped down onto them and made its undulating way over to the row of eggs. Its last word hissed through the cave, seeming to echo louder and louder in my ears: "*Extinction.*"

I suddenly felt very, very tired. "Again?"

*

The second I'd dragged Jake out of the cave, I pulled out my phone and sent a quick message to Lettie at Guardians HQ. I'd hoped for some acknowledgement of the fact that I was actually following procedure for once and reporting a creature encounter right after it happened, but all I got in return was Lettie's usual businesslike "Understood. Tagging team is on its way."

Which really should not be a person's reaction to a text reading: "Giant centipede monster in cave at these coordinates." But since Lettie's whole job was taking in reports from Guardians on whatever dimension-crossing creatures we'd found creeping into the world, I figured shock wasn't an emotion she did anymore. Giant centipede monster? Okay. Sentient mushrooms have infiltrated the farmer's market? Sure. Those dark clouds rolling in are actually mist creatures trying to blot out the sun and destroy all life on Earth? Why not?

I had a moment of wondering if I should mention the centipede's weird prediction to Lettie, but in the end, I decided against it. Whatever my scaly new friend might say about the clairvoyant powers of its species, the truth was that the end of the world was always being predicted somewhere by someone, and none of them had been right yet. It seemed pretty unlikely that a nine-foot centipede hiding out in a cave in Western Pennsylvania would turn out to be the true prophet of the end times.

Jake woke up when we were halfway to the edge of the woods. I'd been dragging him along behind me, and despite the fact that Guardian training kept me in pretty decent shape, it was still no easy task hauling my unconscious, not-so-little little brother across the forest floor. It was late September, but the weather still clung stubbornly to warmer temps, and I was definitely sweating under my T-shirt and light jacket. I kind of hoped Jake felt every rock from the dark depths of unconsciousness. And maybe he could, because one minute he was a 145 pound rag doll, and the next he was fighting his way out of my grasp and letting out an inventive string of curses.

"What happened?" he said after he'd run out of swear words. He sat on the leaf-strewn ground, one hand pressed to his head.

"Oh, I don't know. Maybe you tried to steal a giant bug monster's eggs and it almost killed you?"

He winced and scrubbed his hand over his eyes as if to block out the memories. "Damn, those things were eggs? No wonder it was so ticked off."

I shook my head and gave him my best older sister glare.

Jake Howard, sixteen years old to my seventeen, was currently wearing a tattered denim jacket, baggy T-shirt, and jeans. Like me, he had Mom's dark-brown skin and Dad's big, curved nose, but while my hair sprouted outward and upward in a voluminous pouf, his was cropped closer to his head in loose black curls. Where I was tall and long limbed, Jake was solid and compact, four inches shorter than me and about ten pounds heavier.

And while I had made a sacred vow to protect the world from whatever evil crept in from the fringes of the dark dimensions, he'd apparently made a vow to be as big a pain in my ass as possible.

"Okay, look," I said, dropping down onto the dirt next to him. "I'm not Mom. I'm not going to give you a lecture. But this was pretty nuts, even for you. What's going on with you lately?"

He glared at the ground. "Nothing."

"Very convincing," I said. "Come on, seriously. Talk to me."

He scowled at the dirt for a few more seconds, then sighed. "It's Guinevere."

"Gwen? What about her?"

"I thought..."

"Yeah?"

There was a long pause, and then the words rushed out. "I thought she'd like it. One of those glowy globe things."

"One of the eggs, you mean?"

"Yeah."

I tried not to laugh, as that probably would not have been well-received by my grouchy, love-struck little brother. "Well," I said, "that was a nice thought. And I bet she'd have really appreciated that. You know, until the egg hatched into a baby centipede monster and tried to eat her face."

"I know. I know!" Jake slammed his fist into his thigh. "I get it, okay? I screwed up. I'm a loser, just like Mom and Dad are always saying."

"They've never said that."

"Maybe not, but I bet they're thinking it. I mean, jeez, Alisha, you're out there saving the freaking world, Aggie's getting straight As at college, and what am I? Just some freakishly handsome loser with no girlfriend and no *life*."

My lips twitched upward. "I was wondering how long it'd be before you mentioned how handsome you were."

He managed a slight grin. "I can only hold it back for so long."

"Look," I said. "You know damn well that you're an awesome guy. And while you might not have Gwen as your girlfriend, half the school is in love with you. It's disgusting."

This time, the grin was nearly full wattage. "It is disgusting, isn't it?"

"Horribly, vilely disgusting." I patted his shoulder and got to my feet. "Now, if you're feeling better, can we get out of these woods and get back home? Mom'll kill us if we're late for dinner. Aggie's girlfriend's coming over, remember?"

"Oh, man, is that tonight?" He searched his wrist for the watch he wasn't wearing. "What time is it?"

"Almost five now."

"Crap."

We hustled through the trees and managed to skid in through the front door of our little white house just as Mom was setting the table. She looked up when we entered the dining room, and she was smiling—probably in deference to Aggie's girlfriend, who didn't yet know this woman was capable of Old Testament levels of wrath—but I could see the rage simmering in her eyes.

"Just in time," Mom said. She arched a perfectly sculpted eyebrow at us. "Just."

Mom was beautiful, with smooth dark skin, big brown eyes, and high cheekbones. Her hair was buzzed close to her head, both for style and so it didn't get into whatever she was painting. She wore her silver hoop earrings, a silky patterned shawl, and her favorite black dress with chunky heels. Fun but formal and showing off that whole innate sense of style that had absolutely not passed on to me.

Evidence: while Mom looked ready for the runway, I was wearing scuffed sneakers, jeans, a black *Return of the Jedi* T-shirt, and my favorite worn brown jacket. I far preferred them to any fancier duds, but it did sometimes make me wonder how sure we were that Mom and I were actually related.

"Sorry we're late," I said. "We lost track of time."

"*Almost* late," Jake said, apparently not sensing his extreme danger in saying this. "It's five twenty-nine. We've got a whole minute to spare."

Mom gave us a sweet smile laced with poison. "Of course. A minute is more than enough time for you to get cleaned up, changed, and back down here in time for dinner, isn't it?"

Yep, she was pissed.

"And Alisha, what have I said about bringing that to the table?"

Out of sheer habit, I'd deactivated the magic of the sword clip the second I got into the house, and thus sword and sheath were now both eminently visible hanging from my belt. "Whoops."

"Put it away." She threw a meaningful glance toward the living room, where I could hear laughter and voices—Dad, Aggie, and Aggie's girlfriend, I assumed. "And Jake, take off that torn-up old jacket and put on something fit for company. We'll talk about this later."

Jake and I exchanged wincing glances, but in the end, there was nothing for us to do but obey our mother. Sometimes, no matter how old you were or how many dimension-hopping hell-beasts you'd booted off the planet, that was all you could do.

*

Our older sister, Agnes, despite having been my first instructor in the ages-old art of sarcasm, was also one of the nicest people in existence, fully ready to do anything for the people around her. As such, she tended to attract two kinds of people—jerks who wanted to take advantage of her, and other poor souls who were as tragically, helplessly nice as she was.

Thankfully, Mabel seemed to be one of the latter. She was plump, half-Pakistani, and absolutely adorable, with a cute, upturned nose and freckles. And for all that she was having dinner with her girlfriend's weird family, she was smiling and laughing and managing to make charming small talk like a pro. And not once had she dropped her fork or spilled gravy all over the place, which I definitely would've done in her position.

"So," Mom said in the honeyed voice she reserved for company, "you two met in art class, then?"

"We got paired together for portrait drawing," Mabel said with a grin at Aggie.

Aggie returned the grin with interest. "Yeah, at which point we discovered that we both have old-lady names. It was the first thing we bonded over."

Dad let out a guffaw and choked on his potatoes, while Mom's smile went frigid.

"Agnes was your great grandmother's name, as you well know. Your father and I decided to honor her memory by giving you her name."

"Hey, don't drag me into this," Dad said, using his napkin to wipe some potatoes out of his sandy mustache. "I wanted to name her Sarah Jane."

Mom rolled her eyes. "Honestly, Barry, wanting to name your daughter after some character in a bad sci-fi show."

Dad and I both bristled, as the word "bad" should never tread within a hundred yards of *Doctor Who*.

"Now, listen," Dad began, but Aggie, with her usual flair for peace-keeping, cut in before he could continue.

"Mom, you know I love my name. Great Grandma Agnes was a great lady, and I love that I get to carry on her spirit with my name." She reached over to cover Mabel's hand with her own. "Anyway, if you hadn't named me Agnes, Mabel and I might never have gotten together, so that just makes me love it even more."

The two of them shared a sappy—but adorable—smile, and the tension at the table evaporated.

"Well," Mom said, and her smile actually seemed genuine this time, "more potatoes, anyone?"

Chapter Two

Jake and I got stuck with dish duty after dinner, which wasn't particularly surprising given that Aggie had company; Dad had shut himself up in his study, muttering something about "work to do;" and Mom was still pretty mad at Jake and me for waltzing in to dinner at the last possible second.

"You know Dad's not doing any work in there," Jake said as he swiped a dish towel irritably over a plate. "He's probably watching stuff on Netflix or something."

"My money's on Tumblr," I said. My hands were buried deep in warm, sudsy water, and for all that this was supposed to be a punishment, it was actually kind of relaxing scrubbing the dishes clean. "Fueling his man-crush on Benedict Cumberbatch, I bet."

Jake made a face. "Man, our family's so weird."

"That includes you too, little brother."

"I know it," he said. "But *man*, our family's weird. I mean, jeez, we show up all dirty and roughed up after a fight with a freaking bug monster, and does Mom even ask if we're okay? Nope, just bitches us out and makes us do the dishes."

"Well, you know Mom. She likes to keep her worry buried deep down under a façade of icy rage. It's her defense mechanism."

"Whatever," Jake said, showing—as usual—zero appreciation for my more profound moments of psychological insight.

We were nearly done with the dishes when the doorbell rang. There was the usual "who could that be?" mutter from my mother as she headed for the door, but I knew she'd be all smiles and politeness when she greeted whoever it was. I heard the door swing open—

"Alisha!" Mom called.

I gave a start and nearly dropped the plate I was washing. Who would be coming to see me at seven o'clock on a school night? If it was Guardian stuff, this couldn't be good news.

Exchanging a puzzled glance with Jake, I set off at a jog for the front door—and stopped short in the entryway. There, shaking the rain off his tan overcoat, was a tall, lanky man with graying blond hair and a pair of glasses perched on his nose. His pale face was lined with years of worry, but it was still the kindest face I'd ever seen.

"Uncle Lucas!" I cried, and despite my usual attempts to act my age, I couldn't help launching myself forward and giving him a tight hug.

He laughed and fell back a step, his arms wrapping around me. "Good to see you too, kiddo." His voice was as mild and good-humored as the rest of him.

"God, you're even more skin and bones than usual," I said as I released him. "I think one of your ribs just cut me. What are you doing here? I thought you were off doing important stuff in Bolivia or somewhere."

"Argentina," he said. "And I was."

"Then what are you doing back here? You said you were going to be gone for a year at least."

His brow creased, and I realized that what I'd thought was just his usual tired look was actually something deeper and darker. "I promise I'll explain everything, but for now I need to speak to your father."

I frowned a little but nodded. Adults had been keeping things from me for my entire life, but Uncle Lucas had always been honest with me. If he said he'd explain later, I knew he would.

"Yeah, sure, he's in his study."

Uncle Lucas gave a twist of a smile. "Netflix?"

"Tumblr, I think."

"Here, Lucas," Mom said, uncrossing her arms and stepping forward. "Let me take your coat."

Uncle Lucas smiled and handed over the coat, and Mom smiled as she accepted it, but instead of a warm interaction between a brother-in-law and sister-in-law, it was more like two robots acting out what humans were supposed to do in this situation.

"Thanks, Helen," Uncle Lucas said, and with one last tired smile at me, he headed down the hallway to Dad's study, leaving a dark trail of raindrops in his wake.

After he'd gone, Mom stood staring after him with a deep frown creasing her face, so I took his coat from her and hung it carefully in the closet.

"Mom, why are you like this every time Uncle Lucas comes over?"

Her voice was cool. "Like what?"

"You know 'like what.' Like you can't stand him, or— I don't know, like you don't trust him or something."

She pursed her lips and shook her head with an unmistakable air of *No Comment*, then gave me a sharp look. "Don't you have dishes to wash, young lady?"

I rolled my eyes. "Back to the kitchen, Cinderella."

*

Much later, well past ten, Uncle Lucas emerged from Dad's study, and he and I had a chance to talk. We did so in the kitchen, sitting at the table with our hands curled around steaming mugs of tea.

Uncle Lucas looked even more exhausted than he had earlier, the lines around his eyes and mouth unusually pronounced. He leaned over his cup and let the warm steam wash over his face and fog up his glasses.

"What kind is this?" he murmured.

"Monkey-picked oolong," I said, and his eyebrows shot up.

"This stuff costs a fortune. Are you sure you want to waste it on me?"

"Please, I think you're the only person in the world who loves tea more than I do. If anybody deserves ridiculously expensive monkey tea, it's you."

His lips twitched into a grin, and he took a sip of the tea. His eyes closed in bliss, and some of the lines smoothed from his face.

I waited until he'd had another few sips, then folded my hands and leaned forward.

"All right, now spill. What's going on? Why'd you come back from South America, and what were you and Dad talking about for so long?"

Uncle Lucas took one more sip, then set down his cup and spent a moment studying his fingers. "How much do you know about what I was doing in Argentina?"

"Not much. I know you were doing some kind of research, but Dad was never very clear on what exactly you were researching."

"There are some holy men and women in the forests of Argentina," he said. "They claimed to be able to communicate with spirits, beings from another plane. Which isn't an unusual claim, but what was unusual was that these holy people needed to be in a certain physical location in order to contact the spirits. From the description, it sounded like it might be a weak point in the dimensional wall."

"Another one?"

"That's what I was sent to find out," Uncle Lucas said. "It took some time for them to accept my presence among them, and even longer for them to let me join them for their ritual. Finally, though, I was allowed to accompany them, and they took me to their holy site, an old cave deep in the forest. When we got there, they sank into a kind of trance state, and they did seem to make contact."

"With who?"

The shadows under his eyes seemed to grow deeper. "What do you know about the dark dimensions?"

I felt an icy prickling on the back of my neck. There were so many dimensions out there, most of them populated by beings more or less like us—corporeal, basically decent, and more interested in their own comfort than in making trouble for other worlds. But the dark dimensions were something else. We didn't know that much about them, except that the beings from them were different. Wrong. I'd heard stories about whole planets being decimated by creatures from dimensions like that.

"I know enough," I said. "You think these beings were from one of the dark dimensions?"

"Yes. And the fact that they've made contact with people from this world is worrying to say the least. What's more worrying is that their message to us was clear: 'Open the gate. Let us in.' They were sending instructions, Alisha. They were teaching these holy people how to open a hole in the dimensional wall. How to open a gateway between our world and theirs."

My eyes widened. "Isn't that what happened before?"

"That is exactly what happened before."

While it wasn't something anyone would learn in a history class, it was a story Guardian cadets were taught on day one. A hundred-some years earlier, the first dimensional rift had opened in our world. Or, rather, it had been opened by some misguided human who'd made contact with a being from another dimension. Thankfully, he'd been interrupted before he could finish the necessary ritual to open a full-on dimensional gateway, but when the rift he'd opened slammed shut, the energy discharge had blown him to little bits, and had nearly destroyed the people who'd come to stop him.

Those people, as it happened, later became the founders of the Guardians. The energy discharge from the aborted spell had weakened the dimensional walls, and cracks had formed in random locations all over the world, making it easier for beings from other dimensions to creep into our plane of existence, sometimes for benign reasons and sometimes not. It was the Guardians organization's job to make sure those creatures existed peacefully here on Earth, and if they didn't, it was the job of Guardians like me to make sure they went right back to where they'd come from.

I sighed and folded my hands on the tabletop. "I mean, it's definitely not great that these creatures were trying to get those holy guys to open a gateway, but we've dealt with that kind of thing before. If they come through, we'll just fight them off and send them back."

"In this case, that may not be so easy. If these creatures are what we think they are—they're different. We won't be able to fight them with traditional means, and if they make it into our world"—he met my eyes—"we could be facing literal extinction. The end of life as we know it."

The words hung in the air between us, echoing in my mind in chorus with the words of the centipede monster. I was dimly aware of other sounds in the house—Jake, Aggie, and Mabel playing video games in the living room, Mom moving around upstairs, frantic typing from Dad's study. It all seemed very far away, and suddenly precious.

"I don't mean to scare you," Uncle Lucas said gently. "I just thought you deserved to know what we could be up against. In all likelihood, this will blow over like most threats of this kind do. Even if these creatures do manage to make contact with someone again, they would need someone both close enough to a weak spot in the dimensional wall and strong enough to cast the spell to open a gateway. The Guardians are keeping an eye on all the dimensional weak spots we're aware of, and most of the world's strongest spell casters are either already a part of the Guardians organization or are being kept under close surveillance.

"But I don't think it would be a bad idea for us to keep our eyes open, and to be extra cautious from now on. And that, unfortunately, means it would probably be best not to go off on your own anymore."

I sighed. "But it just takes so long to get permission and backup and stuff. It's so much easier to just deal with things myself."

"I realize that," Uncle Lucas said. "And I know you can take care of yourself—no one's doubting that. But given the circumstances, I think it would be best if you don't try to take anything on by yourself from now on. At least bring your counterpart with you."

I made a face. "Belladonna? But she's the worst. I mean, really, I know it sounds like I'm exaggerating here, but I'm not. She is the *worst*."

"You don't have to like her," Uncle Lucas said with a mild smile. "You just have to be able to count on her in a fight. And from what I understand, she's one of the highest ranked Guardians in the area. Not as good as you are, I'm sure, but still very good."

"Oh, sure, I see what you're doing. Flattering me into being compliant. I get it."

Uncle Lucas reached across the table and rested his hand on mine, his blue eyes soft and pleading. "All I want is for you to be safe. Please, Alisha, promise me you won't go off on your own anymore. Not until we've dealt with this."

There was real emotion in his voice, and I felt a sudden lump in my throat. "Okay," I said. "Sure. I promise." We went back to our tea for a time, and I let the thoughts spin through my head, trying to make sense of them. After a while, one rose to the surface and demanded my attention. "Are we telling Mom about this?"

Uncle Lucas looked uncomfortable. "She's not technically part of the Guardians anymore, and this is protected information. But I do think she has a right to know."

"Yeah," I muttered. "I was afraid you were going to say that."

Chapter Three

I wasn't looking forward to talking to Mom, so I kind of...didn't. I went straight to bed after my talk with Uncle Lucas, and the next morning, I grabbed an early breakfast and hustled off to school before Mom was out of the shower. Cowardly? Yes. But I wasn't even sure what I was supposed to tell her, and I needed some time to figure it out. Plus, it probably wouldn't hurt to let her cool off over the whole late-to-dinner/sword-in-the-dining-room thing before I heaped another layer of badness on top of it.

Anyway, with Uncle Lucas back in town, Mom had to know something was going down, even if she didn't know exactly what it was. And for all I knew, she'd cornered Dad last night and demanded to know what was up, so maybe I wouldn't need to talk to her at all.

Right. And maybe Belladonna wasn't awful after all, just tragically misunderstood.

I parked my bike in front of the school and chained it up, even though I was pretty sure no one was going to steal a flowery pink and yellow bike from the dawn of freaking time. It was Mom's old bike, which she'd kept in prime condition all these years so as to have an excellent reason to say "no" when I begged to be allowed to drive to school like everyone else in my class. *"Why waste the gas when you can just take my old bike to school? It's only a fifteen-minute bike ride."*

So while my fellow juniors zipped around in their or their parents' cars, I was stuck pedaling along the side of the road, my hair trapped under an unflattering bike helmet and my mouth clamped shut to avoid inhaling bugs.

"Hey, Howard," said a voice behind me.

I made a face and with great dignity removed my helmet and re-arranged my hair. When I was satisfied I looked reasonably presentable, I turned.

"Belladonna," I said.

Daisy Belladonna Rodriguez, stupidly named and an even bigger pain in the butt than my brother, stood on the sidewalk in front of the school, keys dangling from her fingers as if to make sure I knew she didn't have to resort to pedal-power to get to school every morning. Her glossy black hair was perfectly styled and curled, framing an annoyingly pretty olive-skinned face that was all soft curves and expert touches of makeup. While I had the look of a fawn learning to walk, no matter how hard I trained, Belladonna looked like an athlete—the shoulders under her soft white sweater were broad, and I knew from covert glances in the locker room that her arms and legs were taut with wiry muscle.

And she was smirking at me. God, I hated that smirk.

"Did you want something?" I asked coolly.

"Obviously," she said in her low, dry voice. "You don't think I'd get this close to you unless I absolutely had to, do you?"

"Then spit it out so we can go back to ignoring each other." I pulled a piece of gum out of my pocket, unwrapped it, and popped it into my mouth to avoid meeting her eyes. I promptly choked on my own spit and had to spend a moment hunched over hacking before I could breathe again.

When I'd blinked the tears from my eyes, I saw Belladonna was regarding me with what I chose to deem concern but which was more likely disdainful amusement.

"Well," she said, arching one slender eyebrow. "Don't you think we should talk?"

"Talk? Us?" I shuddered. "About what?"

"You know, danger on the horizon, dark creatures trying to enter our world— Any of this ringing a bell?"

I stared at her. "How do you know about that?"

"Did you hit your head or something? My mom's head of the council. How do you think I know?"

"I know your mom's head of the council. How could I not, when you mention it every five minutes? But you're just a Guardian."

"Yeah, and so are you, but your dad and your uncle tell you what's going on, don't they?"

"Fine," I muttered because she was right, and I hated her even more when she was right. "The world might be in serious danger. I still don't see what you and I have to talk about."

"We're Guardians," she said, her face going suddenly serious. "If something bad is coming, we need to be ready to stop it."

"Fine. Right. You're right." The words left just as nasty an aftertaste in my mouth as I'd expected, but I plowed on heroically. "What did you have in mind?"

"Meet me after school," she said, and the smirk came blazing back.

"My house, if you can handle pedaling up all those hills. We'll talk then."

And before I could say anything, she turned and headed for the front doors of the school, sliding a massive pair of headphones onto her head that had probably cost more than my mom's car. I rolled my eyes and made sure my helmet was safely strapped to my bike, mostly just to give her time to get as far away as possible before I followed.

What had I done to deserve Belladonna? Seriously.

*

I'd been thirteen when I first joined the Guardians. A minor fuss had been made over the fact that the usual recruitment age was fourteen, but given that my mom was a former Guardian, I'd been taking martial arts classes since I was four, and almost my entire family was entangled with the organization in some way or another, an exception had been made, and I'd joined up the day after my thirteenth birthday.

If anything, I'd wanted it to happen sooner. I'd spent every birthday between nine and twelve begging to be allowed into the ranks, until even Aggie had politely and kindly asked me to shut the hell up and be patient.

Mom had disapproved, because disapproving of things I wanted to do was at least three-fourths of her momly job description, but Dad had been 100 percent on board, and Uncle Lucas had been cautiously encouraging. He'd encouraged me to be cautious, in any case, and had reminded me ten or twenty times that not everyone is cut out to be a Guardian, and if I found it was too strenuous or dangerous for me, there was no shame in deciding to get a job on the research side of things instead, like he had.

But I'd known even then research wasn't for me. I wanted to be on the front lines, kicking monster butts and keeping the world safe. That was what heroes did, right? And that was what I knew I was going to be: a hero.

That all changed on my first day of training, when fate and a particularly sadistic Guardian training instructor paired me with Belladonna.

I was tall and scrawny and full of energy, but Belladonna at age fourteen was already built like an irritatingly attractive brick house, and she had me on the floor within about two seconds of our first sparring match. Which would've been bad enough, but while she was wrenching my arm up behind my back and grinding my face into the mat, she'd hissed into my ear, "How's it feel, Howard? To know that you're not so special after all, and Mommy isn't going to come save you?"

I'd snarled out that I didn't need my mom to come save me and had used all of my strength in a heroic attempt to twist out of her grip and slam my foot into her face. All I managed to do, however, was dislocate my own shoulder and end up in a whimpering pile on the mat.

Belladonna had looked down at me with her perfect lips curling. "God, you're even more pathetic than I thought."

The trainer had apparently agreed, and I'd been sent off for medical treatment and a "reevaluation" of my fitness for Guardianhood. So, yeah, a less than stellar first day. I'd had to work my butt off to keep my position, and while I'd eventually managed to fully join the ranks of the Guardians, I'd still never beaten Belladonna in a sparring match, which was one of those things that crept up into a person's consciousness at three AM and made interactions with Belladonna about a thousand times more irritating. She never said the words, but every time she smirked at me, I could hear a singsong chorus of, *I'm better than you are, I'm better than you are.* I sometimes wished the Guardians would get the memo and give us new counterparts, but for all that we hated each other, we unfortunately worked really well together in the field.

"Damn Belladonna," I muttered, and realized, only as I heard my own voice, that I was sitting in fourth period, tapping my pencil with increasing force on the edge of my desk.

"Alisha," Mr. Akhtar said wearily.

"Right," I said. "Sorry. Paying attention now. Go ahead."

"Thank you," was the dry reply, and I forced myself to push away memories of the past in favor of focusing on Algebra. I was going to end up with a headache either way, so it might as well be for frowning over fractions rather than reliving my past failures.

*

"A giant bug monster's egg." Gwen gave me that flat, amused look she was so good at. "Seriously."

We were sitting at the lunch table, picking at our respective cafeteria meals and trying to pretend there was something even remotely appetizing about soggy spaghetti noodles and peas drenched in marinara sauce.

I grinned. "I'm sure it seemed like a good idea at the time. Until the thing started attacking him anyway. I'm telling you, he's got it bad for you. Not that he's exactly alone in that."

Miss Guinevere Ahmadi arched an eyebrow at me, oblivious as usual to her general hotness. I mean, really: she had the smoothest skin I'd seen outside of a photoshopped magazine cover. Her hair was long, wavy, and shiny (and currently dyed a vivid shade of violet), and beneath her white T-shirt and sequined skirt, she had a body the majority of male students—and yes, many of the female ones—felt no shame in lusting over.

But she had no idea. I could understand how she could feel that way, given her history, but seriously, girl, look in a mirror.

"Right," Gwen said in her low, husky-sexy voice. "Guys are just falling over themselves to get to me. That's why none of them ever even speak to me."

"You intimidate the hell out of them," I said. "I mean, jeez, you're built like an Amazon, and you're gorgeous, not to mention smart. No wonder they're scared to death when you so much as glance at them."

Gwen batted her long eyelashes at me, a lock of purple hair flopping over her forehead as she tilted her head. "Sure it's not you who's into me instead of your brother?"

"Nobody would blame me if I was," I said, which was true. "And we *would* look awfully pretty together."

"We sure would," Gwen said, twining her arm with mine and smiling. "But as we've already established, I think of you as just a friend, and I do believe you see me as the same."

"That's right. You are, and always will be, my friend. My hot, hot friend who my brother is hopelessly in love with."

Her smile slipped, and I knew what she was thinking before she said it. "You think he'd still feel that way if he knew?"

I shrugged. "It might throw him for a loop at first, but I don't think it'd freak him out too much. I mean, the guy faced down a centipede monster for the sake of getting you a big glowy paperweight. If that's not love, I don't know what is."

Gwen looked down at her plate, a flush rising in her cheeks. "I do like him. He's a nice guy, and I can't deny I think he's pretty hot."

"That's one thing you guys have in common, then." I gave her a gentle nudge with my shoulder. "If you like him, tell him. He'll be thrilled."

"Until..."

"Until nothing. Look, you can't hide from this stuff forever. I know how scary it is, having a secret that could get between you and whoever you end up falling for. I mean, I have to find somebody who's okay with me running off to fight monsters every other second. But when you find the right person, they're going to love you no matter what, and nothing's going to get in the way of that."

She gave me a doubtful look.

"Nothing," I said again. "Now eat your mushy noodles before they congeal."

She made a face but shoveled a forkful of the stuff into her mouth. I braced myself, then followed her lead.

"If only it were Ramadan," Gwen said wistfully. "Fasting wouldn't seem so bad when this was the alternative."

"At least tomorrow's taco day," I mumbled through a mouthful of noodley mush.

"Right," she said, and we both took long, long drinks from our beverages.

A hand gripped my shoulder, and I caught a whiff of cologne so strong I nearly had a coughing fit.

"Hey," Jake said, giving me a wide grin. "Mind if I join you, ladies?"

Gwen averted her eyes and took a hurried sip of her water, and I turned to my brother. Aside from the cologne explosion, I could see he'd slicked back his curls with an ungodly amount of gel, leaving his hair stiff and greasy, and instead of his usual comfortable baggy ensemble, he was wearing a snug black tee, a gaudy silver chain, and jeans so tight I doubted he'd be able to sit down.

"S'up, Gwen?" As I watched in horror, he pulled out a pair of sunglasses and slid them on. "Hey, girl. S'up?"

Gwen, quite understandably, choked on her water, and while she was clearing the fluid from her lungs, I excused myself and dragged my brother off by his arm.

"What?" he said, staggering after me in the fastest stiff-legged trot his too-tight jeans would allow. "What the hell, Alisha?"

"Jake." I took him by the shoulders so I could stare directly into his eyes. "As your sister, it's my duty to tell you when you're looking or acting like a complete tool, and I'm afraid that right now, it's tool city."

Jake pulled off the sunglasses and gaped at me. "No. Come on."

"Seriously, this isn't you. My loving sisterly advice is to immediately go to the bathroom and wash that stuff out of your hair, scrub off as much of the cologne marinade as you can, and put on some pants you can actually walk in. Those things are going to split the second you try to sit down, and the whole cafeteria does not need to see your underpants."

"But—" He cast a surreptitious look at Guinevere, then dragged me a few more steps away by my shirt sleeve. "—you wanted me to give it a go with Gwen, right? So that's what I'm doing. She's super into fashion, so I figured I'd try to look more, you know, fashionable. And maybe she'd be into that." He looked down at himself and sighed. "Gwen's a special girl. I want to wow her, you know?"

I squeezed his arm. "You don't need to wow her. Just be *you*, okay? I promise that'll be enough." I turned him around and marched him toward the door. "Now, go change back into my brother, okay? I'll tell Gwen you have something you want to talk to her about, and if you ask her out, I'm pretty sure she'll accept."

Jake's eyes lit up, and he nearly crashed into a sophomore with a full lunch tray as he spun around to face me. "Really?"

"Really. Now get going. I don't even want to think about how long it's going to take you to peel those jeans off."

Jake grumbled something, but he looked pretty pleased as he tottered off in the direction of the boys' bathroom. Back at the table, Gwen was hiding a smile behind one perfectly manicured hand. She gave a smothered laugh as I sat next to her.

"What was that all about?"

"Yet another attempt to woo you, milady. I told him to go wash off all the hair gel and most of the cologne, then come back and ask for your hand properly."

Gwen paled a bit at the words, but I gave her a stern look.

"Gwen," I said firmly. "You like him. He likes you. You know you'll regret it if you don't at least see where it might lead."

She stared at me, and I remembered the night she'd told me. We'd been at her house having a sleepover, and she'd pulled an old photo out of a drawer and shown it to me. A little boy with cropped hair and Gwen's face had stared back at me, looking sad and uncomfortable in a pair of red swimming trunks with arms crossed protectively over a flat, scrawny chest.

"It never felt right." She spoke so softly I could hardly hear her, *her finger tracing almost tenderly over the photo. "Even back then, I always knew it wasn't me."*

"You have to take that leap someday," I said gently.

The uncertainty on Gwen's face melted away, and I was glad to see something like determination take over her expression instead. "All right," she said. "I'll do it. But if this goes badly—"

"I take full responsibility," I said, raising my right hand solemnly. "And you may deal with me accordingly."

"Fine," Gwen said, and a smile peeked through her attempts to look serious. Her hand wrapped around mine and gave it a warm squeeze. "Thanks."

"That's what I'm here for," I said lightly. "Encouragement, support, and occasional butt kicking when needed."

She gave my hand one more squeeze before releasing it, and when my brother returned with damp hair, a less aggressive scent, and pants that actually fit, Gwen got to her feet with a smile and went with him. They talked together in low voices as they walked away, and I watched them with a mix of satisfaction and a tiny prickle of sadness. I didn't intend to have a freakout about my brother stealing away my best friend—or vice versa—but it was hard not to feel a little lonely when two of the most important people in my life were finding love while I was...well...not.

But hey, there was an afternoon at Belladonna's house to look forward to, right? The pain of my utter lack of a love life would pale in comparison to the agony of spending more than two minutes in her company, I was sure.

Chapter Four

After school, I checked my Guardian email to see if any last-minute meetings or training sessions had been called that would tragically prevent me from biking over to Belladonna's. Alas, no such luck. The only message I had was the usual hourly alert letting the area Guardians know where all nearby Non-Earth Beings could presently be found, along with a handy color coding on whether the NEBs in question were staying in their assigned zone (blue), getting dangerously close to the border of said zone (yellow), or strolling down Main Street causing chaos and panic (red).

I was surprised to see there was no dot at all over the centipede monster's cave, and I sent a quick text to Lettie about it—very important and worth delaying my departure over. She replied almost immediately with "Creature had gone by the time tagging team got there. Cave abandoned."

That made me frown, but maybe the centipede had decided to find some cozier spot to welcome its young into the world. Or maybe it had taken its own prediction seriously and was getting the heck off this world before something terrible happened. There wasn't much I could do about it either way, so I filed it away under "huh" and moved on with my life.

All the other dots on the map were safely blue, which was more bad news. If there'd been any yellow or red, I would've been honor-bound to go check it out and possibly schedule a Guardian-style eviction, but the planets didn't seem ready to align in my favor today.

As I snapped on my helmet and got onto my bike, I comforted myself that at least I wasn't a member of the tagging team. Having to go around implanting GPS trackers on a bunch of grouchy NEBs did not sound like fun, but at least it made it a lot easier to make sure the creatures were honoring the staying-in-this-dimension agreement of keeping out of view of the general populace. And let's face it, they probably could've gone walking (or crawling or slithering) down Main Street in broad daylight, and everyone would've just said, "Oh, must be some weird publicity stunt," or "Wow, check out that cosplayer" and then gone back to posting pictures of their coffee cups on Instagram. People were happier not knowing about all the weirdness and scariness that existed in the world, and some days, I really couldn't blame them.

I pulled into Belladonna's driveway sometime later, gasping and covered in sweat. The hills, as she had so hilariously predicted, had indeed been a bit too much for my pedaling power, and I was now well and truly exhausted and looking like a wilted flower to boot. Not wanting Belladonna to see me as anything but cool and in control, I ducked behind a conveniently large flowering bush to get myself in order, and it was at least a full minute before I got my breath back and my hair settled to the extent I felt ready to be seen.

I pushed my flowered bicycle up Belladonna's white cement driveway, trying as I went to ignore the picturesque fountains, the koi pond, the perfectly landscaped lawn, the pillared front of the three-story house, and the general nauseating affluence of the place.

I made it to the front door unmolested by suspicious gardeners asking what a peasant like me could be doing in such a place, and a press of the doorbell sent a pleasant melody chiming through the house. Other than that, there was no sound from inside, and as the moments ticked by with no answer to my ring, I started to wonder if this had all been some trick of Belladonna's to get me to ride all the way up here for nothing.

At last, I heard movement from inside, and the front door swung open to reveal my nemesis herself, clad in a black sports bra and workout shorts and with a towel hanging around her neck. Her dark hair was pulled back into a ponytail, and I was annoyed to see a display of perfectly tight and chiseled abs above the waistband of her shorts.

"Finally made it, huh?" Belladonna said.

"I took the scenic route," I said with a glare.

"Just as well. It gave me time to get in another workout."

We stood there for another few seconds, and it dawned on me that she was really, truly going to make me ask. I parked my bike over on the far side of the porch and gave her a weary look. "So, can I come in, or should I just leap in through the nearest window?"

She smirked and took a step back to let me pass. "Shoes over here, so you don't track anything on the carpet. I would say, 'Make yourself at home,' but I'm not sure you'd know how to do that in a place like this."

I redoubled my glare but didn't take the bait, and eventually she shrugged and led the way through a carpeted, wood-paneled entryway and into what appeared to be some kind of elegant sitting room. Plush chairs and couches were arranged in a way that looked more stylish than functional, and there was no TV in sight, something that would've caused a certain mutiny in the Howard household.

"Have a seat," Belladonna said. "Maybe avoid the white furniture. Those pieces are so hard to clean."

I lifted my chin with all the regality of my mother in full ice-queen mode and lowered myself onto a pristine white sofa.

Belladonna actually looked pleased, a hint of a grin touching her perfect features. "I was wondering how long you were going to just stand there and take it. You're a lot more fun when you fight back, you know."

Before I could figure out how to respond, she turned on her heel, tossed a few words over her shoulder about getting changed, and left the room. And with that, I was alone in Belladonna's immaculate sitting room, seated stubbornly on a delicate white couch, and wondering what the hell I was supposed to do with myself until she got back.

I sat. I looked around at the white walls and the muted colors of paintings whose subjects were far too artful and sophisticated to be recognizable as anything but random blobs of color. I thought about how my mom's paintings were about a thousand times better and probably cost about a thousand dollars less. I sat some more. In the distance, a clock chimed the hour softly, as if not wanting to disturb anyone, and I wondered how many more chimes I would hear before Belladonna deigned to return.

Finally, I decided I'd waited long enough and got to my feet. The house seemed deserted, and for all I knew, Belladonna could be halfway through a luxurious hour-long bubble bath upstairs, so I decided I had no choice but to do some friendly snooping. And if Belladonna didn't like it? Well, it was her own fault for leaving me alone in her house.

I wandered from room to room, taking in a richly furnished dining room, a pristine kitchen with stainless steel appliances and marble countertops, and what appeared to be some kind of sunroom complete with wall-to-wall windows, elegant seating, and a veritable jungle of potted plants. After ducking my head into nearly every room on the first floor, I ended up face-to-face with a conspicuously closed door. I gave the customary making-sure-no-one-was-around glance over my shoulder, then turned the knob and slipped inside.

It looked like another sitting room, but unlike the one I'd been waiting in, it had an air of disuse. There wasn't exactly a layer of dust on the furniture or anything, but the curtains were drawn, and there was a strange sense of stillness to the whole room. At first, I couldn't understand why, and then my eyes were drawn to a framed picture hanging on the far wall.

It was a large, portrait-style photo of a fifteen- or sixteen-year-old girl. She had Belladonna's dark hair and olive skin but an un-Belladonna-like expression of warmth in her large brown eyes. She wore a long, velvety black gown she didn't seem entirely comfortable in, and she'd been posed awkwardly on a hard-backed wooden chair I assumed was a precious antique. Her eyes weren't fixed on the camera but slightly off to the left, and I wondered what she'd been looking at or thinking about when the picture was taken.

While I'd never met this girl, I knew exactly who she was. She was Belladonna's older sister, Mari, who had disappeared five years earlier.

I hadn't been in the Guardians yet when she'd vanished, so I hadn't really known Belladonna at that point—not that I could claim to know her all that well now—but there'd been a lot of talk about Mari's disappearance at school, and of course the local news had been all over the story. I still wasn't clear on the details, but the official story was that Mari had left the house one evening and never come back, and not a soul had seen her since. I kind of half wondered, now, if something other-worldly had been involved in her disappearance, but I had to concede that even people who came from Guardian families could get kidnapped or run away from home.

For the first time, it occurred to me to wonder how Belladonna had been affected by her sister disappearing like that, but I stopped myself before I could go too far down that road of thought. It did, however, make me feel suddenly guilty, like I'd been reading Belladonna's diary or something, so I hurried out of the room and closed the door softly behind me.

Good thing, too, because I'd only been back in the other sitting room for a minute or two when Belladonna swept inside in a flowing black halter dress that reached her ankles. Her hair was twisted up into a bun that beautiful people liked to describe as "messy," but which would've taken most lesser mortals three stylists and two hours to imitate with any success.

"Well, let's get down to it," she said, suddenly all business as she lowered herself into a pale-blue armchair across from me. I shifted my brain out of musing about Belladonna's lost-sister mode and tried to focus on what she was saying. "Something is trying to get into our world, and we need to stop it."

"Okay," I said. "Yes. Agreed. How exactly?"

"Before I tell you what I'm thinking," Belladonna said, "why don't you tell me what you think we should do?"

I glared at her, because it was pretty clear her only reason for asking was because she knew I didn't have a clue. "There doesn't seem to be much we can do. The dimensional weak spots are being guarded, anyone with any strong magic ability is being watched, and we're keeping an eye out for any sign that these beings are communicating with other people on Earth. Doesn't seem like there's much for you and me to do in all that."

"And what if I told you that there might be a weak point in the dimensional wall right here in town, and no one is watching it because nobody knows about it?"

I frowned. "I mean, if that were true, then I'd really wonder how *you* knew about it."

Belladonna smirked. "Asking the right questions for once. Never mind how I know about it. The point is that it's here in town, and we're going to go check it out."

"Why?"

"Honestly, Howard, I know it's hard for you, but think: if no one is guarding it, then it would be a perfect place for those creatures to try to break through."

"Yes, thanks, I got that part. I mean, why us? Why not tell the council or your mom and let them deal with it?"

"What, are you afraid to go check it out yourself?"

I snorted, because recklessly running off to do something on my own was kind of my specialty. "No. But what exactly are we planning to do when we get there anyway? If it really is a weak spot, then it'll need to be guarded, and I'm pretty sure you're not suggesting we go set up camp there ourselves for the rest of our lives."

"We are going," she said, enunciating every syllable as if I was hard of hearing or not particularly bright, "to check it out. It might not even actually be a weak spot, in which case we would've wasted everyone's time by telling them about it before we were sure."

Which was a good point, but something still seemed off. I couldn't figure out Belladonna's game here. She was rarely this intense, and yet her eyes were blazing and her fingers were clenching and unclenching over the fabric of her dress. Why did she want to go to this place so badly?

"Before I agree to go," I said carefully, "I'm gonna need just a little more information. How do you know about this weak spot? Where is it?" *Why is it so important to you?*

For the first time, I saw a flicker of uncertainty in her expression, but it was chased away by another flare of annoyance. "Look, I told you. It doesn't matter how I know about it. But I will tell you where it is."

"I guess that'll make getting there a lot easier, at least."

"There's a cave. It's off a walking trail, but nobody goes in there because there are signs all around warning about cave-ins."

"Well, then, please, let's charge right in there."

"There aren't really any cave-ins. I think people just sensed something strange about the place and put up those signs to stop anyone from going inside. Trust me, I've been in there, and the place is solid."

"You've been inside?" I asked.

Her eyes widened like I'd caught her in something, and she glared in my general direction without meeting my eyes. "Yes, but it was a long time ago. I'm not even sure— I'm not sure it's really a weak spot, but something weird was definitely going on in there, so I think we should check it out."

There was a strange note of desperation in her voice, so I said, "Yeah, all right. Sure. Let's go check it out. When do we go?"

"Tomorrow after school. I'll pick you up in the school parking lot."

"Oh, you mean you don't want me to drive? You could sit up on my handlebars."

Belladonna gave a cool smile. "Thanks, but I'll pass. Right after school. Don't be late."

*

I was pretty sure Belladonna was out of her rich little mind, but I had to admit, I liked the idea of doing something a heck of a lot better than sitting around waiting when the end of the world might be on its way. I figured I should probably tell Dad or Uncle Lucas what we were planning, but when I even mentioned the idea, Belladonna sank her claws into my arm and hissed that we were telling *no one*. Which seemed like a big ole red flag that what we were doing was a bad idea, but I figured we couldn't get into too much trouble just checking out an old cave.

After all, we were Guardians, and this kind of stuff was what we were supposed to do. I mean, generally we were supposed to wait until we were ordered to do it, but why waste HQ's time with something that might turn out to be nothing at all? And I *was* technically keeping my promise to Uncle Lucas. He'd told me not to do anything by myself, and I wasn't. Model niece and general all-around trustworthy individual, that was me.

By the time I got home, it was just about dinnertime, and the house had settled into that pleasant predinner routine of Dad stirring a pot in the kitchen, Aggie playing video games in the living room, Mom holed up in her studio painting, and Jake—

Jake, I discovered, was not in his usual place at the table waiting not-so-patiently for dinner but was instead up in his room with some cheesy love ballad from the nineties blaring. I rolled my eyes but couldn't help grinning as I knocked on his door. And then knocked again, more loudly.

Bryan Adams stopped just short of telling me who he was doing everything for, and the door swung open.

"God, look at you," I said with a laugh. "You have the dumbest smile on your face. I guess things went well with Gwen?"

Jake nodded, looking dazed but happy. "She said she's liked me for a while, but she wasn't sure how I felt."

"And here I was sure everyone from here to Pittsburgh knew how you felt."

"Shut *up*," he said, but the impact of the words was lessened by the huge grin that accompanied them. "Anyway, we're going out tomorrow night, and I'm really happy about it, and so thank you for helping me and telling me to go for it, and that's all, so see you at dinner. Bye."

The door closed—gently—in my face.

I grinned and headed downstairs, while Bryan Adams began to sing soulfully from my brother's room again.

Dad raised his sandy eyebrows at me as I walked into the kitchen. "Do I even want to know?"

I laughed as I got the dinner plates down from the cupboard over the sink. "Jake finally asked Gwen out."

"What?" Dad said. "*No*. And she said yes?"

"Shockingly, she did."

"Well, no wonder Jakey's taking us on a tour of nineties love ballads, then. And what's up with you, kiddo? How was Belladonna?"

I froze with a plate halfway to the table and threw him a suspicious look over one shoulder. "How do you know I was with Belladonna?"

He gave an innocent shrug of his shoulders. "I'm your father. I'm all-knowing and all-seeing."

"Dad."

"Martina Rodriguez is head of the council, my dear. That house is under constant surveillance. The Guardian data team knew you were there before you even rang the doorbell."

I flushed and went back to setting the table. "Belladonna wanted to talk about some stuff."

"Mm-hmm," Dad said, making a failed attempt at sounding casual. "And what kind of 'stuff' did she want to talk about?"

"Just stuff." I felt a little weird about not telling my dad what Belladonna and I had talked about, but at the same time, I couldn't help thinking he'd try to talk me out of going to the cave if he knew, and I really wanted to go. I could practically see it playing out in my head: Belladonna and I went to the cave, and we were just in time to see some nasty creatures trying to break their way through the dimensional wall and into our world. Poor Bella got knocked out in the first five minutes of the inevitable fight, and I had no choice but to bravely save the world myself and forever secure my place as an amazing Guardian far superior to my poor, unconscious, weakling counterpart.

A girl could dream anyway.

"She just wanted to talk about doing some extra training," I went on as I dug through the silverware drawer. "You know, so we can be ready in case something bad does end up going down."

Dad was quiet for a moment, stirring his pot of pasta. "Very sensible. And it's good to see you and Bella getting along."

"We're not friends," I said, lest he get the wrong idea. "I still can't stand her, and I know she feels the same about me."

"All the more impressive, then, that you're getting along. Dinner's almost ready. Think you could rally the troops?"

I set off through the house to sound the alarm, and I couldn't help feeling a hot twist of shame at hiding what we were doing from my dad. I did my best to ignore it, and before long it got the idea and faded away.

Chapter Five

"You're kidding," I said.

Belladonna sighed and pushed her oversized sunglasses on top of her head. All around us, kids streamed by on their way to get to their own cars or walk home after school. A few cast envious glances at Bella's car, or maybe just Bella herself. "Just get in," Bella said.

I was far from an expert in the wild world of automobiles, but even I could see that this car was *nice*. It was a sporty white convertible with a shamelessly red interior and a general look of being the kind of vehicle to ferry good-looking multiracial young people to the beach while pop music played. I opened the door and slid carefully into the seat, where my bare legs promptly stuck.

"Buckle up. I'm not getting a ticket because you're too dumb to fasten your seat belt."

"Aye, aye," I said, rolling my eyes as I tugged my seat belt into place.

"And if we pass anyone I know, duck down and pretend you're a pile of clothes," Belladonna said with a smirk. She stamped on the gas pedal, and we were off.

We roared out of the school parking lot and promptly got stuck waiting at a light, which I enjoyed simply because it seemed to irritate Belladonna so much.

"So, what's the plan?" I asked.

"Go to cave, enter cave, check it out."

"I see. Spent a lot of time on that one, huh?"

"Sometimes simple is best." She threw a sidelong glance at my plain gray V-neck T-shirt and shorts. "Sometimes."

"Yes, I'm a poor peasant in poor peasant clothes. Let's move on. Probably we won't find anything in this cave, but just in case we do, do we have weapons?"

"In the trunk. Extra swords, an axe, a bow, and arrows. Do you shoot?"

"I'm gonna say 'No.'"

The smirk returned. "Too bad. I'll handle the archery if it's needed, then."

"Communication?"

"Earpieces. Connected to each other in case we get separated, but with long range capabilities if we get into serious trouble. But I doubt we'll find anything we can't take care of ourselves."

"Yeah, I mean, the end of the world can't be more than the two of us can handle, right?"

Belladonna gave me a cool look. "I doubt we're going to find the end of the world in there. But if we do, I'm sure we can handle it. Have a little faith. If not in yourself, at least in me."

I snorted. "Sorry."

We sped on in silence for a while, and I had to admit that it felt pretty great to be riding through the unseasonably warm September afternoon with the wind rushing through my hair and the seat firm and comfortable against my back. Even Belladonna's presence couldn't disrupt my good mood, and I wondered why I should be feeling so uplifted when we were heading into a potentially dangerous situation without telling anyone we were going. But on a sunny afternoon, it was hard to take any of it seriously. I mean, the end of the world couldn't possibly happen on such a nice day, right? Logic.

About twenty minutes later, Belladonna eased us to a stop on a dusty pull off, and we got out of the car. We were at the start of a scenic trail along a low, rocky river, and while a few cars passed by on the nearby road, no one else seemed to be around.

Bella was already digging through the trunk. She pulled out two duffel bags that clinked suspiciously when they hit the ground.

"I made yours a little lighter so it won't be too tough for you to carry," she said, and I couldn't help noticing the flex of her wiry biceps as she lifted her own duffel and slung it over her shoulder. I wondered if she'd worn a tank top today just for the purpose of showing off how obnoxiously fit she was. "We wouldn't want you getting tired out before we even get there."

"Thanks ever so," I said. I got my assigned duffel bag on my shoulder with a quick, casual motion that would've been a thousand times cooler had the contents not slammed into my back and momentarily knocked the wind out of me.

Bella snorted and shook her head. "Honestly, you are too easy sometimes."

I glared at her but followed her onto the trail because where else was I going to go with a duffel bag full of weapons? The trail was dusty but well-maintained, trees and a steep hillside rising on one side while the river lapped and burbled along on the other. As we went on, trees crowded in on both sides, and soon we were walking through a sunlit tunnel of leaves that still hung on to summer green despite autumn being well on its way. Birds twittered, the air was warm and fragrant, and the quiet bubbling of the river was decidedly tranquil.

"This would be kind of nice," I said, "if I were here with somebody else."

"Mm, I was just thinking the same thing," Bella said easily. "If the world doesn't end, I'll have to come back here sometime."

"Maybe have a picnic," I said.

"Definitely."

We exchanged grins, and then I realized I was sharing a joke with Belladonna and looked away with a shudder. "How much farther to the cave?"

"Not too far. We should be coming up on the entrance in a few minutes."

I tried to get my mind into potential battle mode, but it was tough when the surroundings insisted on being so peaceful and idyllic. Still, I managed at least to screw my face up into something that might've looked vaguely tough, though more likely the look I achieved was closer to "constipated" given the weird glances Belladonna kept giving me.

"That's it," Bella said a few minutes later, pointing at a dark hole about midway up the rocky hill to our left. It was, as promised, surrounded by signs warning of cave-ins, and the path up to it was rocky and nearly vertical.

"Glad I wore my sneakers," I said.

"Do you ever wear anything else?"

I opened my mouth to retort, but I was distracted by Bella pulling something out of her pants pocket. As I watched, she unfurled a pair of fingerless climbing gloves and slipped them on.

"Seriously?"

She flexed her glove-clad fingers at me. "It pays to be prepared." Then, sighing, she pulled another pair from her other pocket and threw them at me. They bounced off my face and fell to the dirt, and I waited for one dignified second before bending down to retrieve them and pull them on.

Climbing the rocks was much easier with the gloves, and we made it to the top without incident. Bella had gone first, which meant I got to enjoy having pebbles and bits of dirt kicked onto my face as she climbed, but if anything were an apt metaphor for every moment I spent with Belladonna, that was it. Just something to be accepted and dealt with like any natural disaster.

Finally, we stood at the mouth of the cave. A gray coolness seeped from it, smelling like dark and dank and stone, and a hush fell over the world as we stood there, as if the birds had stopped singing, or we'd ventured beyond the reach of their song.

"Nope, not creepy at all," I said.

Bella was digging in her duffel bag, which she'd set on the wide ledge we stood on. "Get suited up. There's armor, weapons belts, and your earpiece in the bag."

It was a little tricky, the two of us getting on our gear on a rocky ledge fifteen feet from the ground, but we managed it. Bella, of course, did so far more quickly and gracefully than I was able to. I wondered vaguely what we would do if some random hiker came strolling by on the trail below, but luckily, no one else seemed to be around.

A few minutes later, I looked down at myself with some measure of satisfaction. The thick black vest fit snugly over my torso, and the thigh and shin guards strapped over my legs gave me an extra feeling of security and protection. I'd strapped an axe to my back, handle upward, and of course I had my sword in its golden clasp on my belt. The axe was pretty heavy, and I couldn't help wishing it were possible to have more than one magically sized-down weapon. But the magics always interacted badly, and neither enchantment worked right as a result. It made me suddenly glad for all the Guardian training exercises that had required us to go on long jogs through the woods with heavy weapons.

Bella, meanwhile, wore the same kind of armor but had a bow and a quiver of arrows on her back and nothing but a long, slim, katana-like blade at her belt, not enchanted at all, just hanging there in all its samurai glory. She was in the process of tucking her earpiece into her ear, so I followed suit and inserted mine, making sure to turn the thing on first, as that was a mistake I'd made more than once in training missions before, to the great amusement of all, especially Belladonna.

When Bella's eyes met mine, there was none of the usual haughtiness to them. She looked somewhere between exhilarated and terrified.

"Ready?" she asked. She'd tapped her earpiece before speaking, and I heard her voice echo in my ear.

I tapped my own. "Ready."

With one last glance at the perfect sunny afternoon behind us, we slipped into the cave.

Chapter Six

As one would expect from a cave, the interior was dank and dark. I dug my mini flashlight out of my pocket—and realized after clicking it on and off a few times that the batteries had chosen this exact moment to die. Awesome. I was just wondering if I should break out my cell phone and shine the screen around like a dope when Bella switched on a tiny flashlight of her own and tossed another one to me. I managed to catch it, not disgracing myself for once, and we shined our lights around the cave walls.

"Not much to see," I murmured.

"Not so far. But we're barely past the entrance. It goes a lot deeper than this."

We walked in silence, and I thought I'd never really heard silence before this moment. Except for the faint scuff of our feet on the cave floor, the world was filled with a vast, screaming nothing. It pressed and pulsed in my ears and made me feel weirdly suffocated, and I could see from the faint frown on Bella's face and the way she tapped her ear from time to time that it was bothering her too.

At first, the cave was barely big enough for both of us to walk in, the walls close and the ceiling forcing us to bend forward to avoid scraping our heads. As we went deeper though, through endless curving tunnels, the cave opened up and we were able to stand upright and leave a bigger gap between us as we walked. More space would make it easier to fight if we had to, at least.

We'd been walking for what felt like a thousand years, but which was probably only six or seven minutes, when something changed. It wasn't something I saw or heard, but something I felt, and Belladonna felt it too because she stopped at the same moment I did.

"Did you feel that?" she whispered.

I nodded, not daring to speak. I could *still* feel it. All the hairs on my arms stood on end, and the air buzzed with an almost electric charge. The hum of the silence now seemed like an actual hum coming from somewhere ahead of us, and so with an uneasy exchange of glances, Bella and I crept forward.

We came to what was, unmistakably, a doorway in the righthand cave wall and, just as unmistakably, a flicker of light from beyond it. We approached with all the stealth and caution of two well-trained Guardians and at last drew close enough to peer past it into the chamber beyond.

I almost gasped out loud. Beyond the raggedly carved doorway was a large, squarish chamber of the same gray stone as the rest of the cave. Candles were placed at various locations around the room, flickering softly and casting weird shadows on the walls. And sitting cross-legged in the center of a circle of candles was my dad.

Bella's fingernails dug into my arm, warning me against moving or saying anything, but I was too shocked to even remember to breathe, let alone speak.

Dad sat very still, his eyes closed and an air of deep concentration about him. Then there was a rustle of fabric, and I realized he wasn't alone.

"Are you sure you're not dragging your feet on this just a bit?" said a cool, lightly accented voice, and I felt Bella go rigid beside me.

We stared at each other, for once no trace of animosity between us, then turned back to see what the hell our parents were doing surrounded by candles in a creepy cave.

Martina Rodriguez had always intimidated me and most likely would've done so even if she hadn't been the head of the whole Guardians council. While my mom had the bearing of an icy queen, Martina was more like a fiery empress, tall, regal, and burning with some strange inner fire. She was a few years older than my mom, definitely past the age when she would start getting gray hairs, but she'd dyed her dark hair a vibrant red as if to cast out any signs of age or weakness. Her hair was short and straight, kept trimmed to just below her ears, and it framed a face that was olive-skinned and heart-shaped like Belladonna's, with dark, thick-lashed eyes and features that looked carved out of stone.

As she walked closer to my dad and his circle of candles, I saw she was wearing some kind of ceremonial robe, dark blue and dragging softly along the cave floor. Her red hair was like a flame in the light of the candles, and the shadows playing on her features made her look even more intimidating than usual.

"These things take time," my dad said, and at the sound of his familiar, comforting baritone, something in me relaxed a little. Whatever might be going on here, it couldn't be bad if my dad was in on it, right? I mean, jeez, he was sitting there in a polo shirt and khaki shorts, for crying out loud. You couldn't be secretly evil when you dressed like that. "You do want this done right, don't you?"

"Of course, I do. And I know that if anyone's capable of doing it, you are."

Dad's bushy eyebrows lifted. "Well, I'm flattered."

"Don't be. Just get on with it."

Dad nodded with his usual easy compliance and got back to whatever he was doing, his eyes closing and the look of concentration returning to his features. Martina, meanwhile, loomed over him, arms crossed and a definite air of impatience radiating from her.

Dad opened his eyes to give her a sideways glance. "Must be hard being back here." His voice was light, but I could sense a heaviness in the words. "You sure you want to do this?"

Martina glared at him, the expression bringing out the resemblance between her and Belladonna for an instant. "Very sure."

"Because there's no guarantee this'll work, you know."

"I'm aware of that."

"And given the situation, now might not be the best time to try it."

"Now may be the only time we can try it," Martina snapped. "With the news your brother brought back from Argentina, the Guardians are going to be on high alert, and they will be looking particularly hard for undiscovered dimensional weak points. It's only a matter of time before they find this one, and then it will be under guard all day every day, and we'll have no chance of getting this done. So please, let's just do this and worry about the consequences later."

"All right," Dad said easily, though he looked taken aback by the outburst. "Whatever you say. And I'm ready whenever you are. You have the binding spells ready in case this goes wrong?"

"Of course."

"All right, then, let's give this a go."

Dad closed his eyes again. His lips were moving in some sort of murmuring chant, his voice getting louder and deeper as the moments crept by. Martina had taken a few steps away from him and stood staring at the far wall, which I could now see was scarred and blackened as if it had been burned.

The chanting continued, getting louder and louder, and the hairs on the back of my neck decided to join the hairs on my arms and come to attention. A rush of wind swept past me and swirled around my dad. His sandy hair flapped around his head, but he kept his eyes closed and continued his chant.

Bella's nails dug into my arm again as the blackened part of the cave wall started to glow faintly blue. As the glow intensified, it became clear that the charred place on the wall formed a long, narrow gash, like someone had slashed a blade through the stone. And that gash was growing. As it stretched wider, from a finger's width to a hand's width to two hands', the wall behind it shifted to translucent and I could see shadowy shapes pressing up against it from the other side, trying to push their way through. Martina drew closer to it, holding her hand out as if to touch the creatures beyond, and I heard her murmuring something to the shadows as if beckoning them closer.

A jolt of pure terror went through me. This was the weak spot in the dimensional wall, and my dad and Martina were trying to *open it*.

"Dad, no!" I shouted, bursting into the chamber despite Bella's attempts to restrain me.

And that was when it all went wrong.

Dad broke off mid-word, as you would if your daughter suddenly burst in on you as you chanted mystical incantations in a cave. I suddenly remembered all the horror stories about interrupted spells, particularly powerful ones, but it was much too late now. Martina jerked back from the wall as the glow around the gash changed from blue to a dark, pulsing crimson.

"Alisha?" Dad gaped at me. "What are you—?"

"No time for that," Martina said in a tight voice. "They're coming. Barry, get the rift closed again as fast as you can. I'll do containment in case they get through."

The wall was now as transparent as glass, and the shadows I'd seen grasping from beyond were pushing their way through as if breaching a thin, stretchy membrane. My hands shaking, I grabbed for my sword, aware even as I did so that Belladonna had come up beside me and was holding her bow out in front of her, an arrow cocked and pointed at the wall and the creatures crawling out of it.

"Foolish children," Martina snapped at us, "those won't do any good."

She still stood by the gash in the wall, but she had drawn back a step or two and placed herself carefully between us and the creatures. My dad had returned to his chanting, a bead of sweat creeping down over his forehead, and I couldn't understand how he could bear to keep his eyes closed when those things were so close to breaking free.

"What *are* they?" Bella said under her breath, and I shook my head wordlessly.

I'd thought they were flesh and blood creatures, but they weren't. They were shadows; they were air; they were ghosts? I didn't know how to describe them, but two of them had nearly squeezed all the way through the gash in the wall, while Martina stood fearlessly in front of them, one arm extended, palm outward, as if to stop them with sheer force of her will alone. If anyone could do it, I thought shakily, she could.

And even though she'd said weapons wouldn't work against

whatever these things were, I kept my sword lifted and at the ready, and I saw out of the corner of my eye that Bella was doing the same with her bow. We glanced at each other and gave a tight nod. Whatever might happen here, we would at least go down fighting.

My dad's furious chanting reached a crescendo, and the gash began to glow blue and inch closed. The wall rippled with gray as if beginning to change back to a plain cave wall again—

And the creatures broke free.

Two black shadows surged out of the wall and flew straight for Martina. She was ready for them, shouting a word and making a gesture like she was throwing something at them, but they dodged whatever it was and soared free around the cave. It had never been clearer to me that weapons were not going to work on these things, but I still took a swipe at one of them when it passed me. It moved through my sword like smoke, and I could've sworn I heard it laughing as it swept by.

When Dad finished his chant, the rift closed, and the wall became a wall again. But the two shadow creatures were swirling around the room too quickly even for Martina to get a hold of them, and I wondered with some alarm just what these things could do to us to make the head of the council and my own father so afraid of them.

Martina shouted a few more words I couldn't understand, and this time, she must have hit her mark, because a pale, bluish glow surrounded one of the shadows like a cage and held it in place. It gave a high-pitched scream and shuddered in its bonds, but it couldn't get free. Martina gave a tight smile—

And the other shadow slammed into her from behind and disappeared inside her body.

Bella and I froze, and even my dad went still, his eyes locked on Martina. Her body had gone rigid, her arms outstretched at her sides and her eyes closed, her head tilted back. She began to shudder, and Bella gave a strangled cry and tried to rush forward. I grabbed her arm and managed to hold her back.

Dad looked from Martina to Bella and me with a helpless, sorrowful look on his face, and then he lifted a hand and spoke a few words, and Bella and I were propelled out of the chamber and back into the cave tunnel. We hit the ground hard, and by the time we'd crawled to our feet, the doorway shimmered as if an invisible wall had sprung up there. Bella and I rushed forward, trying to get to our parents, but whatever barrier my dad had put up stopped us. We were left watching helplessly as Martina's eyes opened and she stared around the cave chamber with an utterly alien look on her face.

"Good," she said. Her voice was deep, dark, and unquestionably not her own. "This will do nicely."

"What happened? What's wrong with her?" Bella shouted, tears streaming down her face as she tried to push through the shimmering barrier. "Mom!"

"Alisha, honey, listen." It was my dad. He looked exhausted, swaying where he sat, and I wondered how much energy closing the rift in the wall had taken from him. "The other one's going to get me too. I don't have the strength to hold it off. And when it does, the barrier will come down, and I won't be able to protect you. You and Bella have to run, do you understand? Run and tell your mother what happened, and your Uncle Lucas. And you don't need to mention to Lucas that he was absolutely right about this being a bad idea because it's pretty clear now that it was."

I felt like I might start hyperventilating but managed to speak anyway. "Dad, what's going on? What do you mean, the other one's going to 'get' you? What's happening?"

Dad turned to look at me, and all I saw were kind blue eyes and a sandy mustache as his mouth curved into a soft smile. "I love you. I'll try to get back, but if I can't... Make sure your mother and your brother and sister know how much I love all of you. I'm sorry it turned out this way, kiddo."

I opened my mouth to ask, again, what the hell he was talking about and why this sounded like a goodbye, but by this time Martina had walked over to where the other creature shuddered in its blue cage and, with a snap of her fingers, released it. It hovered there for an instant, seeming to exalt in its sudden freedom, and then it surged forward and disappeared into my dad's chest. His head snapped back and he gave a ragged yell that echoed through the cave and deep into my bones, and I slammed myself forward against the barrier.

"Dad!" I shrieked.

Bella was grabbing at my arm and babbling, "We have to go. We have to go. *Alisha, we have to go!*"

It felt wrong to run, but I knew we had to. The barrier was already flickering, and God only knew what Not-Martina and Not-Dad would do to us when it came down. Because something had taken them. I knew that now. Something had come through the dimensional wall and taken them over, and I didn't know if that meant they were still in there somewhere or were gone forever, but either way, it wasn't something I was ready to think about.

We ran.

I felt the barrier come down, a sizzle in the air and a burst of static electricity, but I didn't look back, and I didn't think about what was going to be chasing us. Bella and I just kept running.

We made it to the mouth of the cave without anything grabbing us or killing us, and that was a definite plus. But as I was about to follow

Bella out into the daylight, I glanced back at the tunnel we'd come from, and I was just in time to see two white, ghostly wisps come speeding after us. I opened my mouth to shout a warning, but before I could get it out, both wisps flew into my chest and disappeared, and I knew I was doomed.

Chapter Seven

Except, somehow, I wasn't doomed. Nothing tried to take me over, nothing made my body twist and contort in weird directions, and Bella and I were able to make our shaky way down the rock wall and back onto the riverside trail without anything out of the ordinary happening. I started to wonder if I'd imagined it, but I knew I hadn't.

Well, if I was going to be possessed or have my soul eaten from the inside out or something, there was nothing I could do about it now.

"Back to the car," I managed, out of breath and exhausted and scared but knowing we had to follow my dad's instructions or die trying.

"The car," Bella agreed breathlessly, and we took off at a sprint down the trail.

It was still the same day, the same perfect, sunny day that had seemed so untouchable before we went into the cave, but the sun had sunk lower in the sky, giving the light a flat, dying look that warned that even perfect days all ended the same way—night fell, light left, and the world was swallowed in darkness.

Jeez, kiddo, lighten up, came a voice in my head, and I felt a sudden lump in my throat at how much the voice sounded like Dad. Dad, who now was possessed by some weird shadow creature from another dimension because of me, because of what I had done. Dad, who had used his last ounce of magical energy to protect Bella and me, even if it meant sacrificing himself in the process.

"All my fault," I tried to say, but it came out as half a sob. "It's all my fault."

Bella looked back at me with pain in her dark eyes. "It's both our faults, which just means we have to be the ones who fix it."

We staggered to the car a short time later, crawled in, and took off at a speed that would have gotten us arrested if anyone of the police persuasion had noticed. But no one was around, and we roared off in Bella's convertible without anyone seeing us go.

"You forgot your seat belt," I said vaguely as I glanced over at Bella.

"Who cares?" she said.

It occurred to me that I should text headquarters, but I had absolutely no idea what to say. In the end, I tapped out a message to Lettie that read, "Dimensional weak point at these coordinates. Weak point has been compromised by body-stealing shadow creatures. Martina Rodriguez and Barry Howard taken—can no longer be trusted. Proceed with extreme caution."

Lettie didn't reply, and I wondered if, for once, I'd actually shocked her.

*

It didn't seem right that my house looked the same as it always did, a cute suburban two-story with red shutters, white siding, a bright-red door, and a front porch with white wicker furniture. Bella's convertible pulled into the driveway with a crunch of wheels on gravel, and despite the urgency of the situation, we both just sat there in our seats once the car was turned off, staring at the closed garage door and not speaking or moving.

"I guess we have to go in," Bella said at last. Her voice sounded lower and huskier than usual, and I knew she was feeling as torn up inside as I was.

"I guess we do," I said.

Neither of us moved.

"Are we sure that really just happened?" Bella said. "How likely is it that we both just hallucinated that whole thing?"

"Not too likely."

She nodded dully. "That's what I thought."

Bella turned to look at me, and I'd never seen so much fear in her eyes. "Do you think we can get them back? I mean, do you think they're still in there somewhere, or were they...?"

My jaw tightened. "I don't know. But if we're going to do anything to get them back, I'm pretty sure we're going to need to get out of this car."

Bella sighed, and we both climbed wearily out of her convertible.

I'd expected the predinner routine to be in full swing despite Dad's absence, but the house was deadly still when I opened the front door. The lights were off, and the curtains were drawn, so the house was dim and shadowed and entirely too creepy for my liking.

"That's weird," I said, speaking in hushed tones because it felt wrong to speak any louder in the unnatural silence. "They should be home by now."

I took a few steps into the house, aware of Bella pushing the front door shut behind us—

Someone leaped out of the shadows and grabbed me in a viselike grip, pinning my arms to my sides. I struggled and kicked as I was dragged down the hallway, hearing scuffling and a yelp from behind me, but I couldn't break free, and a moment later Bella and I knelt on the soft beige carpeting of the living room. My mom stood above us with her sword pointed at our throats.

"Mom, what—?" I began, but she jabbed the sword at me, and I wisely shut my mouth.

In addition to the sword, Mom wore her old Guardian battlewear, a snug, black, two-piece jumpsuit with a belt for the sword and a pair of sturdy black boots adorning her feet. I hadn't seen her dressed like this since she'd retired from the Guardians when I was twelve, and I couldn't help thinking how much more at home she seemed in these clothes than in her usual everyday outfits.

"Helen, this seems a bit excessive," came a quiet voice, and I twisted my head around to see Uncle Lucas standing behind Bella, his hand outstretched in the same way Martina's had been when she'd tried to capture the wall creatures.

"I didn't ask for your opinion," Mom said. "And we have to be sure. They were in that cave too, and they could've been taken just as easily as— They could've been taken just as easily." She turned her gaze back to Bella and me with a new intensity blazing in her brown eyes. "If you're really my daughter, you'll be able to answer this question. What did I tell you on your seventh birthday?"

I stared at her. "Mom, seriously? I can't even remember what you told me two weeks ago, let alone when I was *seven*. And you probably told me a lot of things that day—it was a *whole day*."

The intense stare continued, so I let out an exasperated breath and struggled to remember. *My seventh birthday, my seventh birthday...* "That was the year I had the chicken pox," I said, the memory fuzzy but coming back to me as I talked. "Nobody could come to my party because they didn't want to get infected, and I was pretty mad about it."

A glimmer of something softer touched Mom's eyes. "Mad is an understatement."

"I threw all my books and stuffed animals onto the floor, and when you told me to clean them up, I said it wasn't fair that I had to clean anything up when I was sick. And you said..."

I fell deeper into the memory and couldn't help smiling a little at the image: A furious, spotty girl sitting in pony-print pajamas on the edge of her bed with her arms crossed, glaring down at the stuffed animal carnage as if it were their own fault they'd incurred her wrath. Mom had knelt beside me so she could look up into my face, and her voice had been soft when she said...

"We clean up our own messes in this house, young lady."

Mom closed her eyes for a moment in relief, but the sword didn't waver in her hands. She shifted it to point just at Bella.

Bella, meanwhile, was looking at me with an odd expression on her face. "She seriously made you clean all of that up when you had the chicken pox?"

I shrugged. "I was the one who made the mess, so I was the one who had to clean it up."

The words hit home for me as soon as I said them, and they must've done so for Bella too because she gave a tight nod and didn't say anything else.

"All right," Mom said, "so it seems like you're still you, Alisha, and as for Belladonna..."

I got to my feet and pulled Bella up with me. "Mom, she's fine. Nothing got to her. Dad— He put up some kind of force field and kept us safe."

"Helen, I think we can trust that these two are all right," Uncle Lucas said.

Mom ignored him. "Belladonna, what did I say to you on the day you were accepted into the Guardians?"

"You said that your daughter was going to be joining up soon, and I should—" She hesitated, and it seemed like she wanted to glance over at me but restrained herself. "I should look out for her."

Mom lowered the sword. "Yes, and what a wonderful job you've done of that."

Bella flushed and looked down at the carpet as if she were ashamed—*ashamed? Belladonna?*—but I didn't have time to wonder at this revelation because suddenly Uncle Lucas was there, hugging me tightly in his skinny arms. "We were so worried about you two. Thank goodness you got out of there all right."

The feel of his arms around me almost made me lose my composure all together and start sobbing about all that had happened and how terrible it was, but I managed to keep a hold of myself. "How do you even know that something happened? And how did you know to check us to make sure we were us? Did Lettie contact you or something?"

"It was your dad," Uncle Lucas said gently. "He was wearing an audio recorder, and he set it to automatically send its contents to me if anything happened to him."

I took a step back from him. "So you already knew he was there? What was he doing? It looked like he and Martina were trying to open the rift, but why would they want to do that?"

An oddly closed expression came to Uncle Lucas's face. "I'm afraid it's not my secret to tell."

"Oh, come on," I said. "You're not really going to give me a cop-out answer like that."

"Yes, he is," Mom said in a hard voice. "And what's more, you have no right to be questioning anyone after what you and Belladonna did today. You went to that cave without telling anyone, you interrupted a delicate and dangerous spell, and now because of you, the head of the Guardians council and our most talented spell caster—your own father, let's not forget—have been compromised."

Instead of breaking me down, the words made me stand straighter and look my mother in the eye. "I know," I said. "And I intend to do everything I can to make this better."

Atta girl, said Dad's voice in my head, and I pushed down another wave of emotion that threatened to rise up.

"I don't know if it's even possible to get them back," I said, "but if we can..."

"That remains to be seen," Uncle Lucas said. I could tell he was choosing his words carefully. "These creatures— They're called the vesu, and when they take over a host, they force that host's spirit out to make way for their own."

Alarm tore through me. "Then where's Dad's spirit? Where did it go?"

"Easy," Uncle Lucas said. "It should still be in the cave. We have people going there now to secure the place, and if—when they find your dad's and Martina's spirits, they'll try to preserve them as best they can until we can get their bodies back. The fact that they're in the cave is encouraging, actually. Spirits don't do well in bright places, especially direct sunlight, so a dark place like a cave is ideal." He hesitated. "I have to tell you though that I'm not entirely sure how long spirits can exist outside of their bodies. If we can't find your dad and Martina in that cave, we might just have to accept..."

"*No*," I said, and I heard Belladonna making similar protests beside me. "We have to find them, then. We have to—"

Honey, you don't have to find me. I'm right here.

"We— We have to— What?"

I'm right here.

Dad. Dad's voice in my head?

I'm here inside of you. Martina too.

I took a shaky step backward. "What? Both of you?"

Bella was eyeing me with some alarm. "Howard, who the hell are you talking to?"

We are both here, came a new voice, cool and confident and with an edge of annoyance. *Trapped in the mind of a seventeen-year-old while our bodies are being used for God knows what evil purpose to bring about the end of the world.*

Well, gee, when you put it that way, it sounds pretty bad, doesn't it? came Dad's dry reply.

I pressed my hands to my ears as if that would help. "No, just— stop! This is crazy!"

"Alisha, what's going on?" Uncle Lucas looked seriously concerned, his hands pressing into my shoulders, and I noticed Mom had raised her sword again and was pointing it in my direction. Not that I could blame her.

"They're in me," I said. I knew I sounded insane, but I also knew that what I was saying was absolutely true. "Dad and Martina. I can hear their voices in my head. Their spirits are in *me*."

Chapter Eight

Mom's sword dropped to the ground, and I was dimly aware of Uncle Lucas ushering me over to the couch and helping me to sit down. Calm blue eyes gazed into my own, and I came back from wherever the shock of it all had sent me.

"Alisha, I hope you don't take this personally, but we need to test this. I'm going to ask you some questions, and please tell me whatever your dad or Martina says in response, all right?"

I nodded, and to my surprise, Belladonna sat beside me, so close I could feel the warmth of her body next to mine.

"This question is for your dad," Uncle Lucas said. "I assume he can hear me?"

Loud and clear, Luke.

I reported what he had said, and a flicker of emotion touched Uncle Lucas's tired, lined face. "Who named me," he asked, "and why?"

I did, Dad said. There was a pause and something like dark amusement in his tone. *After my imaginary friend. Mom and Dad liked the name and decided to go with it despite the fact that it came from a three-year-old.*

Uncle Lucas's lips twitched into a small smile when I told him what Dad had said, and he sat back looking satisfied.

"Next question," my mom said. She sat on the edge of the coffee table just in front of me, her eyes blazing again. "For Martina. What reason did you give me when you asked me to retire from the Guardians?"

There was a long silence from within my head.

Come on, Tina, my dad said, sounding amused again. *Spit it out, or they'll think Alisha's lying about having you in here.*

Fine, Martina said in a cold voice.

My eyebrows lifted in surprise as I met my mom's eyes. "She told you that you should stay home and take care of your kids?"

How's that for feminism, huh? Dad said.

"Seriously, Martina?" I said.

I had seen what neglect was doing to my own children. Martina's voice oddly strained. *I didn't want the same thing to happen to Helen. And I didn't* order *her to leave the Guardians, I merely suggested that she might want to do so before her children—before they got old enough to resent her never being around.*

"Huh," I said.

Bella was looking at me intently. "What? What did she say?"

I shook my head, pretty sure I should keep that last part to myself. "Just something about it being a suggestion, not an order."

My mom snorted. "Yes, Guardian council members are always just making *suggestions*, aren't they?"

"Putting that aside for the time being," Uncle Lucas said mildly, "it does seem as if Barry and Martina's spirits managed to take refuge in Alisha somehow."

"Why only her?" Belladonna said. "I mean, it makes sense for her dad to be in there, but why is my mom there too? Why didn't she— I mean, I was in that cave too."

I could see her trying to sound like she didn't really care, but the hurt in her eyes was clear. "You'd already left the cave when it happened," I said. "They didn't catch up with us until we were right at the mouth of the cave, and I was the only one still inside. It's not safe for them to go into the daylight, so they had no choice but to go into me."

Bella frowned but seemed somewhat satisfied with this. "I guess that makes sense."

Is she actually sad? came Martina's puzzled voice from my head. *Is she sad I chose you instead of her?*

I didn't answer. "All right, so at least now we know where Dad and Martina's spirits are. So what do we do now? How do we get their bodies back and get those vesu things back where they came from?"

Mom looked suddenly troubled. Uncle Lucas put his hand on her shoulder as if to comfort her, but she shrugged it off with a dark look.

"It's likely they're going to try to take over," she said in a hard voice. "They'll open the tear in the dimensional wall again, wide enough so more and more of them can pour through, and then one by one, they'll take over the bodies of everyone living on this planet until they have total control. It's what they do. They're parasites. World destroyers. Every damn one of them."

No one spoke for a few moments.

"Well," I said, my mouth dry. "That sounds pretty bad."

"It's not ideal," Uncle Lucas said. He'd been frowning at my mom, but his expression cleared as he met my eyes. "In any case, our biggest priority is securing the cave so no more of the vesu can come through. After that, we need to get to your dad and Martina's bodies and force the vesu out. There are some rituals I've read about that might be worth trying, but we can't do anything until we find them."

"Where do you think they went?" Bella said.

Uncle Lucas opened his mouth to reply, but a high-pitched squealing noise interrupted him. I jerked, the sound piercing through my brain, and realized I'd never taken out the earpiece in my right ear. The squeal came from there, and as I dug the thing out, the squeal was swallowed in static, and I heard voices and commotion and the unmistakable sounds of steel on steel.

"Waiting for us—" A woman's gruff voice could be heard through the static. "—more of them—tear in the dimensional wall—can't secure the cave—don't trust—"

The voice vanished in a rush of static, and Belladonna and I stared at each other with wide, horrified eyes.

"They got them," I said, but the words from the earpieces must've been loud enough for my mom and Uncle Lucas to hear because Lucas was already rushing out of the room. His voice echoed from the kitchen a moment later, saying, "Grayson, come in. Come in, Grayson. Are you there? Can you hear me?"

"Claire Grayson," Mom said quietly. "Her daughter Kylie—"

"She's in my class," I said faintly.

Mom got to her feet. "We can't stay here. The vesu can't access old memories, but they can see what was on the surface of their host's mind when they took it over. They might come here."

"Where are Jake and Aggie?"

"Your grandmother's house. That's where we should be going too."

"Grandma's? But we haven't been there in years, not since—"

Mom gave me a cool look. "Yes, I know. But family is family, and your grandmother would never turn us away. Plus, it's been long enough since we've been there that I doubt it would be in your father's short-term memory. We should be safe there for the time being."

"But what about everyone else?" Gwen's face flashed in front of my eyes, and the fact that I'd seen her only about two hours earlier seemed insane. "What about the other people in town? They don't know that anything is coming, and what if—?"

"We can't protect them if we get taken too," Mom said. "We need to get to safety, and then we can make a plan, regroup with the rest of the Guardians, and see how bad the situation really is."

"The sun's going down soon," Bella said quietly.

I followed her gaze to the window and realized what she meant.

"They're trapped in that cave right now, aren't they?" I asked. "Grayson said the dimensional wall was torn, so more of them must have come through. And if they're spirits, those vesu things can't come out in the daylight. But when the sun goes down…" I looked to Uncle Lucas as he came back into the room. He looked pale, and I figured he hadn't been able to get in contact with Claire Grayson or any of her team. "Uncle Lucas, Dad made some kind of barrier in the cave. It kept us out and the vesu in. Could we make something like that and put it over the mouth of the cave? Keep them in?"

Uncle Lucas shrugged into his ratty old trench coat. "That's what I'm going to arrange right now, but it won't be easy. Spells like that take a lot of energy to hold in place if someone is actively trying to break them down. We'll have to have someone on duty at the cave all night every night if we're going to stop the vesu from escaping."

"You'll need armed backup too," Mom said. "If Grayson's team was taken, then the vesu have five trained fighters on their side now."

The two of them began to discuss the details, but I didn't hear any more. Bella grabbed me by the wrist and tugged me out of the room, through the kitchen, and into the adjoining dining room. She pulled me to a stop by the dining room table.

"Look," she said quietly. "There's no way to make this any less weird, but...I need to talk to my mom for a minute."

I raised my eyebrows in surprise but nodded. "Yeah. Sure. She can hear you, just talk."

Bella looked away from me, and everything about her was suddenly different. Her posture, her face, everything seemed to belong to a different person, one who was meek and uncertain.

"Look, Mom..." She glanced over at me, then seemed to decide that would be too weird and turned her gaze to the nearest wall. "I need you to tell me what you were doing in that cave. Was it something to do with Mari?"

"Mari?" I echoed in surprise. "Why would it have anything to do with her?"

Bella glared down the floor to avoid meeting my gaze. "Before she disappeared, I followed her into that cave. She was talking to someone, but there was no one else there, and it felt— There was just a weird feeling to that place, and I think now that she might've been communicating with someone through the dimensional wall. It never even occurred to me until your uncle came back from Argentina and started talking about the same thing going on down there, but it would make sense. What it doesn't tell me is what happened to her." She met my eyes again, determination blazing on her face. "Mom, I need you to tell me what you were doing in that cave. I need you to tell me the truth."

There was a long silence from within me.

"Martina?" I said.

I'm here.

"So, are you going to answer her, or...?"

Just give me a moment.

There was a sense rather than a sound of a sigh in my mind, and Martina's voice echoed within me again.

This really is not the time to discuss this, but please tell Bella that I was there in that cave with your father to try to seal the tear in the dimensional wall and prevent any of those things from getting into our world.

I relayed the message, but I couldn't help frowning as I did so. "Not wanting to contradict you," I said, which is something you say when you absolutely want to contradict someone, "but it kind of looked like you and Dad were opening a rift instead of closing it. At the start, I mean."

"Yeah, it did look like that," Bella said in a dark voice. "What were you really doing?"

We were seeing if the weak point could be strengthened, Martina said, and maybe because her spirit was literally existing inside me, I could feel the lie in her words. *But in order to do that, we needed to first open the rift and seal it properly. That's what we were doing. Until, of course, we were interrupted.*

I gave Belladonna a quick summary of that information, and to my surprise, she seemed to buy it.

Martina, I said silently, *I'm sure you have your reasons, but I know for damn sure that was a lie. You were opening that rift for some other reason. It was like you were trying to communicate with the vesu or something. I saw you. I heard you.*

Might as well tell her the truth, my dad said, sounding amused despite the seriousness of the situation. *She won't let up until you do.*

Fine, Martina said. *But we were honestly going to seal the rift back up once we'd finished what we'd come to do.*

Which was?

There was a pause.

Getting Bella's sister back.

My eyes widened, but Bella was spared from wondering what the heck was wrong with me because my mom appeared in the dining room doorway at that exact moment, a look of tense impatience on her face.

"We're leaving in ten minutes," she said. "If there's anything you need from your room, Alisha, you'd better go get it now. And take Bella with you. She can borrow some of your clothes for while we're staying at your grandmother's."

Even though everything was deadly serious and I'd just learned that apparently Mari Rodriguez had been sucked into another dimension, I couldn't help laughing at the horrified expression on Belladonna's face.

"Borrow...*your*...clothes?" she managed.

"Come on," I said, grinning. "Let's go find you a nice sci-fi T-shirt and some ratty jeans."

My mind filled with my dad's laughter, and as I led Bella upstairs, I hoped that someday I would hear it echoing through the house again, not just in my own head.

Chapter Nine

Belladonna stayed near the door of my room, arms folded, as she glanced around in disgust. "I figured it'd be bad, but this is even worse than I imagined."

I threw an old T-shirt at her and deeply enjoyed when it hit her full in the face. "Shut up. There's nothing wrong with it."

And there *wasn't*, I thought defensively. It had your standard twin bed—with starry space comforter, of course—wooden bookshelf packed with novels I'd read a dozen times, desk by the window piled with home-work and textbooks, dresser with framed photos and random memora-bilia on top, and closet with sliding doors in the corner. The walls had once been papered with pictures of cute floppy-haired boys I'd cut out of magazines as a clueless preteen, but I'd since recognized my mistake and now had a poster of Linda Hamilton in *Terminator II* (classic, though it tended to give me major biceps envy), a *Wonder Woman* movie poster (aspirational and highly enjoyable to look at), a beautiful signed photo of Nichelle Nichols in full Uhura getup (a gift from my dad), and—to go from subtle to obvious—a rainbow flag Aggie had gotten me as a coming-out present. It was getting a little faded after two years, but I couldn't see myself ever replacing it.

I opened my closet door and started pulling out the contents, mainly clothes and weapons, and was dimly aware of Bella wandering around my room behind me. When I glanced at her, I saw she was looking up at the rainbow flag, and I turned away, not wanting to hear whatever comments she might have about that. To my surprise, she didn't say anything, and when I looked again, she was over at my dresser examining the family photos lined up there.

"You guys look happy." Her voice was soft as she studied a picture of Mom, Dad, Aggie, Jake, and me taken at an amusement park a few years earlier. We did look happy, arms around one another and big grins on display for the camera.

"Yeah, we were." I remembered riding the bumper cars with Dad, going on a crazy looping roller coaster with Jake and Aggie, and riding some kind of superfast space ride with Mom while she gritted her teeth and clutched her seat and kept her eyes shut the whole time.

"What's it like?" Bella asked. Her back was to me, so I couldn't see her face, but she sounded almost wistful.

I opened my mouth, not sure what I could even say to that, but Bella shook her head as if to cast out the wistful thoughts and turned to me with a hard look on her face. "So, what's the verdict? Find anything I can wear without losing all my dignity?"

"Keep talking like that, and I'll give you my old pink bunny pajamas."

She shuddered and sat on the edge of my bed. "God, anything but that."

After some searching, I found a few items that might not completely repulse a fashion-conscious, teen-model-type like Bella. I tossed them at her and then set about stuffing my own clothes into a duffel bag, along with anything and everything I laid my hands on that might come in handy during an indeterminate stay at Grandma's.

Grandma... We talked on the phone every few months, and always at holidays and birthdays, but I hadn't seen her in years, and how was it that after everything that had happened, going to her house and seeing her again seemed the most surreal of all?

"Hey, Howard?"

I glanced at Bella. "Hm?"

"You're lucky, you know? To have a family like this. One that cares about each other and gets along. You're lucky."

She was looking down at her hands instead of at me, and I was strangely touched by the words.

"Thanks," I said softly. "I guess I am." I hesitated, then asked, "What about...?"

"My family?" She gave a humorless laugh. "It's the usual sob story. My mom never had time for me, my dad left when I was little... Stop me if you've heard this one before."

I got up from my clothing pile and sat next to her on the bed. "Your dad just left?"

"That's what my mom told us anyway. Doesn't matter. Even if he'd stayed, it wouldn't have helped. He and my mom never really got along. I'm pretty sure he married her for her money, and then I guess he realized that even money wasn't worth having to live with—" She broke off and looked at me with wide eyes, as if suddenly remembering that her mother was currently residing in my head and could hear every word she said. "Anyway, he never seemed happy, so if leaving made him happy, then I'm glad he left. I wish I could've gone with him."

She got to her feet. "Look, I'm gonna go get the car ready. You want me to put this bag in the back?"

"Sure," I said, feeling dazed and off-balance. "I'll be down in a minute. I just want to pack one more bag."

She grabbed the packed and zipped bag and headed out, and I was left staring after her wondering what the hell had just happened.

I always knew she was unhappy, Martina said faintly in my head. *But I never knew... I didn't realize she hated me so much.*

"She doesn't hate you," I said. "If she hated you, what you did wouldn't bother her so much. She loves you. You're her mom, and she wants you to love her and be proud of her. That's what we all want, isn't it?"

Martina was silent, and my dad seemed to feel for once that it wasn't his place to interject, so I finished packing and headed downstairs.

*

Uncle Lucas had already left, rumbling off in his battered Toyota, so it was just Mom in her blue Taurus as we made our escape. Bella and I, by unspoken agreement, hopped into her convertible. It was weird, but I actually wanted to be sitting there with her, and I started wondering if maybe I'd been taken over by the vesu after all, because it sure wasn't like me to want to spend any more time with Belladonna than I had to.

The sun burned low in the sky, right at eye level, so Bella slid her shades on, then pulled another pair from the glove compartment and tossed them into my lap. "Here. We might as well both look good."

I grinned and slid them on, and a glance in the rearview mirror confirmed that we both did, in fact, look pretty stylin'. The sunglasses also did a good job of hiding the lingering horror in our eyes, so we were able to ride along without any passersby suspecting we were on our way to hide out from evil body-stealing monsters from another dimension.

Grandma lived out in the countryside on what had been a working farm before Grandpa had died about eight years earlier. It took us about twenty-five minutes to get there, but at least we got some nice scenery along the way, lots of green pastures and trees and the occasional herd of cows chewing and mooing as we sped by. It was nearing dusk by the time Mom pulled into the long gravel driveway, and as Bella and I followed, I glanced up at the darkening sky nervously.

"I hope Uncle Lucas got that cave sealed up," I said. "If he didn't..."

"If he didn't, we'll know about it soon," Bella said.

We'd scarcely pulled to a halt in front of the old, white farmhouse when the door was flung open and Aggie came running outside. The screen door banged against the porch wall, the sound setting off a hundred fond childhood memories, and I felt a little rush of emotion at the thought of finally seeing Grandma after all this time. I'd missed her, and I knew my dad had too. I was pretty sure he'd tried to patch things up with her more than once, but Grandma was a lady who kept her promises. If she said she'd never see us again, she'd never see us again. Except if the world was invaded by shadow monsters, apparently.

"Mom! Alisha! Thank God, you're okay!" Aggie cried, and I'd never been gladder to see my older sister before than I was in that moment. Her curly black hair was secured by two barrettes on either side, her bangs flopping over her glasses as she ran, and she wore her usual untucked button-down shirt with jeans and sneakers.

I leaped out of the car and hugged her, and then I stood back and looked at her like I hadn't seen her in years. I felt like I hadn't.

"How about you guys?" I asked. "Are you okay? How's Grandma? Did Mom and Uncle Lucas tell you what happened?"

"We got the condensed version from Uncle Lucas while Mom was shouting for us to get our stuff and get in the car," Aggie said dryly. She sobered, her dark eyes meeting mine. "Any word about Dad?"

"Uh...yeah." I wasn't sure how to break the news, but I was pretty sure that out in the middle of the driveway was not the best place to do it. "He's okay. We found him. His spirit, I mean. I'll give you the details later."

Luckily, Bella came up behind us at that moment, both our duffel bags on her shoulders and a cautious look in her eyes. I covered the awkward pause by going to take one of the bags off her shoulder.

"Aggie, you remember Belladonna?"

Aggie gave me a look that was politely questioning, but she was all smiles when she reached out to grip Bella's hand. "It's good to see you. I wish it was under different circumstances than our parents getting taken over by creatures from another dimension, but welcome."

Bella's eyebrows lifted in surprise, but a flicker of a smile touched her lips as she shook Aggie's hand. "Thanks." She hesitated. "And, hey, I'm sorry...about your dad, I mean."

"Thanks. I'm sorry about your mom. But hey, these things happen. Well, I guess they don't, usually. But still." She put both her hands over Bella's and gave them a gentle squeeze. "No one blames you guys, you know."

"Pretty sure Mom blames us," I said.

"Almost no one blames you," Aggie amended, giving me a *be quiet now, please* look before returning her gaze to Bella. "Whatever happened in that cave, it was the vesu who did this, and they're the ones who are going to have to pay for it."

The look on Bella's face was somewhere between wonderment and gratitude. She didn't have a chance to answer, however, because my mom—already on her way to the front door with an armful of stuff from the car—called back to us, "Come on, get inside. We can't risk being out here when the sun's down, not until we hear from Lucas."

Aggie, Bella, and I exchanged grim looks and followed, and I stepped through the front door into a world of memories.

It smelled the same—like vanilla and wood and a hint of something else, something distinctly Grandma's house. The door led into a mud room that was also the pantry, and Bella was starting to take off her shoes when Aggie gave her a kind smile.

"No need to take them off unless they're muddy. This isn't that kind of house."

Bella gave her a strange look but kept her shoes on, and we dropped our duffel bags in the corner before heading into the kitchen.

I heard Grandma before I saw her.

"Everybody safe inside?" Grandma's gruff voice had always made me think she must've been a smoker at some point in her life, but Dad had always insisted that wasn't the case. "I'll put the barrier back up if they are."

Grandma stood at the old stove in the corner of the kitchen, stirring a bubbling pot and looking just as I remembered her. She wasn't all that tall, but she was sturdy and comfortable and had eyes that could take one look at someone and know exactly who they were and what they were about. She had on a worn checkered flannel shirt that might've been one of Grandpa's, along with a pair of thick black jeans and boots. Emotion welled up inside me at the sight of her, but after so many years, I didn't feel like I could run up to her and hug her like I had when I was a kid, so I just stood in the kitchen doorway watching her, waiting for her to turn around and see me. Waiting to see what she'd do.

"Everyone's in," Mom said.

Grandma gave the pot one last stir and turned to face us. Her thick gray hair was pulled back in a loose tail, but several strands of it had escaped to frame her tanned, rugged old face. Her eyes met mine, and they were just as clear and piercing as I remembered.

"It's good to see you, sweetie. I'll greet you properly after I get this barrier set up. Won't be a minute."

She disappeared into the other room, and barely twenty seconds passed before I felt a fizz of magic. A glance out the nearest window showed me a pale-blue barrier that glowed there for a few seconds, then faded to invisibility.

"That ought to keep those bastards out," Grandma said, coming back into the room with a look of satisfaction on her face. "I left a back door in there for Lucas, if he decides to join us. Nobody but him'll be able to open it, so we can sleep safe in our beds tonight."

"You're a spell caster too?" Bella asked, and I glanced at her in surprise. She hadn't said a word since we'd walked in, and now she was looking at Grandma with open admiration.

"I am, but let's keep that just between us," Grandma said. "Last thing I want is the Guardians snooping around my farm just 'cause I've got some talent for magic." She came to stand in front of Bella with her hands on her hips. "You're Martina Rodriguez's girl, aren't you?"

Bella flushed at being referred to like that, but she nodded. "Yes, ma'am."

Ma'am? I thought incredulously, but Grandma seemed to like the sound of it.

"Ruth Howard," she said, holding out a calloused hand for Bella to shake. "Strong woman, your mother. Sorry to hear about what happened to her, but I'm sure we'll figure out how to get her back."

At last, Grandma turned to me. She looked deadly serious, and I resisted the urge to take a step back.

"And you, my dear young lady. Much as I've appreciated the phone calls on my birthday and Christmas, I can't help noticing you didn't send so much as a card on Grandparents' Day this year."

I stared at her, shocked that she could actually be upset about something like that—

And then she laughed and wrapped her arms around me and pulled me close. She smelled like fresh air and linen and clean sweat, and she squeezed me so hard I almost lost my breath.

"Lord, it's good to see you again," she said into my ear. There was a catch in her voice that I hadn't heard since Grandpa died. "It's been hard not seeing you all these years or watching you grow up, but it looks like you did a pretty great job of it without my help."

I gave her a good squeeze in return, then reluctantly released her. "Grandma, has there been any word from Uncle Lucas?"

"Not yet, but I'm sure we'll hear from him soon."

"Where's Jake?"

"Upstairs on the phone. Got himself a girlfriend, has he? He's been on the line with her for over an hour now."

"Speaking of," Aggie said, "I should go call Mabel."

Grandma had gone to the stove to stir the pot and check on something in the oven. "All my grandbabies with boyfriends and girlfriends... Well, just girlfriends, come to think of it. How about you, Alisha? Found that special someone?"

I felt my cheeks warming and pointedly did not look at Belladonna, not wanting to see whatever look might be on her face. "Not yet, Grandma."

"Well, that's fine. No point rushing into these things. You want to help me set the table, Alisha? And maybe your friend can help by getting the water glasses out and filled."

"Sure, Grandma," I said, and we got to work. It felt good to be doing something, even something as simple as setting the table, and Bella didn't complain or look like she was judging the rustic dining room with its big oak table and worn wooden chairs. She set out the glasses and filled them from the water pitcher like she'd been doing it all her life.

"I bet this isn't what you thought you'd be doing tonight," I said.

Bella actually laughed. "Not a chance. If I were at home, I'd be—" Her smile faded, and I wondered what she was thinking about. She went back to filling water glasses without saying anything else, and I decided not to push. I was getting the impression, though, that Bella's life was a pretty lonely one, and I couldn't help feeling sorry for her and wishing there was something I could do to help her.

You're already doing it, came Dad's voice from inside me.

What do you mean? I asked silently.

But Dad didn't answer, and I was left to puzzle it out on my own.

*

Dinner had always been a huge deal at Grandma's house, and clearly nothing had changed on that front. We all got scrubbed up and took our places around the big table, Grandma at the head and Mom at the foot. Jake and Aggie took their old seats on the side of the table to Grandma's right while Bella and I took the left. We'd all helped bring in the platters of food, and now they sat steaming on the cheerful red runner in the center of the table, sending out delicious aromas that made me remember I hadn't had a bite since lunch.

"Well, can we eat?" Jake said. He'd finally been persuaded to get off the phone with Gwen, not even giving me a chance to say "hi" to her before he hung up, and now he was fully focused on the platter of mashed potatoes in front of him, fork in hand and ready to dig in.

Grandma gave him a stern look. "I don't know what you do in your house, young man, but in this house, we give thanks before we eat."

Jake looked longingly at the mashed potatoes but nevertheless put down his fork, and we all bowed our heads, Bella doing so a second or two later than everyone else, as if it was the first time she'd ever done such a thing.

Grandma's voice rang clearly through the silence. "We give thanks for this food we are about to receive, and for the fact that all of us are together here today, safe and sound and not taken over by shadow monsters. Let the bonds between us make us stronger so we can take down these bastards, get Barry and Martina out of my granddaughter's head, and keep our world safe. Amen."

The "Amen"s were a bit scattered—Aggie struggling not to laugh, Bella looking confused, Mom gazing heavenward as if saying a prayer of her own for patience, and Jake staring at Grandma with wide, impressed eyes.

Grandma lifted her head. "All right, then, that's done. Let's dig in!"

We dug in. Grandma had gone vegan a year or two after Grandpa died, but her cooking hadn't suffered. We had cauliflower steaks marinated in barbecue sauce, mashed potatoes with gravy, a fresh spring salad with vegetables from the garden, a three-bean salad with fresh herbs, and apple pie for dessert. It was the best meal I could remember having in a long time. No offense to Dad or his cooking skills, but nothing could beat a homecooked meal from Grandma.

We were just starting dessert when we heard something hit the kitchen window, followed by a sizzle and a high-pitched shriek.

We all leaped to our feet.

"Grandma, what—" I started, but Grandma was already leading the way into the kitchen, looking grim but not overly alarmed.

We all piled into the room, Grandma casually picking up a baseball bat from behind the refrigerator as she passed.

Wham. Something slammed into the barrier beyond the glass, and this time, we saw it. It was hard to distinguish from the blackness of the growing night, but when it touched the barrier, the barrier shimmered slightly and gave off a faint glow.

It was one of the shadow creatures. It was one of the vesu.

"Looks like Lucas couldn't keep them in that cave," Grandma said.

"How did they find us?" I asked.

"Could be they're just out and about and trying to get at any house they see."

"Maybe they got Uncle Lucas," Jake said.

"No," Grandma said.

Aggie reached out as if to touch Grandma's shoulder, then seemed to change her mind and let her hand drop to her side. "I know you don't want to believe it, but—"

Grandma's expression was calm. "I'm not saying I don't want to believe it. I'm saying it's not possible. They didn't get Lucas. They might've gotten everybody else, but not him."

The three of us exchanged frowns, but I was the one who spoke. "How can you be so sure?"

"Trust me" was all she said, and then she slipped the bat behind the refrigerator and headed to the table. "Anyway, the creatures are out, but they can't get past that barrier, so we might as well finish our pie. Nothing else we can do for now."

It felt wrong to go eat pie when body-stealing shadows were

roaming the countryside, but even I could see there was nothing else we could do. If we left the house, we'd get taken over in a second, and we didn't have any idea how many of them there were. Grayson had said the dimensional wall was torn, but what did that mean? How big of a tear? How many had gotten out? Were they still getting out? And what had happened to Uncle Lucas?

My stomach was too twisted with worry and fear by this time to even think about dessert, but I filed back into the dining room with everyone else. Mom didn't even sit, just grabbed her phone from the table and hurried off into another room, maybe to try to get in touch with Uncle Lucas or someone else from the Guardians. Aggie and Jake both looked pale and worried, and I knew they were thinking about their respective girlfriends, or maybe just the fact that the whole town could be taken over by the vesu overnight and we'd have no way of knowing or stopping it.

We'd been sitting in silence for a minute or so, Grandma the only one actually eating, when Bella stood.

"We can't just sit here!" she burst out. "We have to do something!"

Grandma eyed her calmly. "What exactly do you think we ought to do?"

Bella's dark eyes flashed. Her hands were clenched into fists at her sides. "Something. *Anything*. We can't just stand by and let everyone get taken over by those things. We have to stop them!"

"We will," Grandma said. "But right now, all we can do is stay safe in here and make sure none of us gets taken. When Lucas gets back—"

"He's not coming back!" The impact of Bella's fist against the tabletop made the silverware rattle. "They got him, just like they got Grayson and my mom and probably everybody else who's even gone near that cave. And you want us to sit here and eat pie while everyone in town gets taken too?"

Grandma rose to her feet. "You're upset, and you should be. It's awful what happened to your mom, and what's probably happening to a lot of others right now. But the second I take that barrier down, those things will rush in here and take every single one of us, and then nobody will be left to fight them. Is that what you want?"

Bella gave a cry of pure frustration and sank into her chair, her head in her hands. I put my hand on her shoulder out of pure reflex, and she didn't shrug it off.

"It's not fair," Grandma said quietly. "It never is. But sometimes you just have to accept there's nothing you can do. And in the morning, when it's light again and those things can't come out, we'll go and see what we *can* do, but for now, we're going to sit and wait and have some pie. If we don't, this pie will go to waste, and wasting food is one thing we don't stand for in this house."

Bella lifted her head and stared at Grandma in disbelief, but Grandma had gone back to her dessert and seemed to be enjoying it. Aggie and Jake followed suit, still looking pale and taking only tiny bites, and I gave Bella's shoulder a quick squeeze before letting go.

"It really is good pie," I said, and Bella looked at me like I was completely out of my mind before sighing and dejectedly picking up her fork.

She took a bite and gave a watery smile. "It *is* good."

Grandma looked pleased, and we finished our pie in silence.

Chapter Ten

"It's weird, isn't it?" Aggie said. "Being back here after so long." She glanced in the direction of the bathroom window as the barrier sizzled again, another vesu trying to pierce our defenses. "I mean, that's not the weirdest thing by far, but still. You know what I mean?"

I spat my mouthful of toothpaste into the bathroom sink. "I know. So much time has passed, but at the same time, it's like no time has passed at all. And Grandma..."

Aggie smiled. "She's still Grandma."

"Definitely," I said, and we laughed.

We were both in our pajamas, sky blue for Aggie and cream-colored with brown polka dots for me. It was hard not to feel like we were kids again, crowding together in the upstairs bathroom to get ready for bed and maybe beg Grandma for a story before we went to sleep.

"Do you ever regret it?" Aggie asked softly.

I could have pretended I didn't know what she meant, but we both knew I did. "I regret what happened. But I don't regret joining the Guardians. Not even a little. This is what I was meant to do, and I know Grandma didn't like it—"

"That's an understatement," Aggie said dryly.

"—but it was still something I had to do."

"I know," Aggie said. "Being a Guardian is part of you, and it always was. It's like you were born to do this. But I understand Grandma's side of it too. I mean, her little brother was a Guardian, and he died because of it. When she heard Mom and Dad were going to let you join up, and at the same age he did—"

"I know. I get it. But hey, it turned out all right, didn't it? I'm still here, and— Well, the world is maybe ending, but aside from that, things are okay, right?"

Aggie grinned. "Right." She sat down on the edge of the old, scratched bathtub and regarded me with something between compassion and amusement. "How are Dad and Martina, by the way? It must be pretty weird, having them both in your head like that."

"It's been an adjustment," I said. "But they've been pretty quiet lately."

Now that I thought about it, I hadn't heard much of anything from them in hours. My pulse quickened, and I set my toothbrush down in alarm.

Dad, Martina, you guys still in there? I asked worriedly.

There was a long pause.

We're still here, kiddo. I never realized how much energy it took to be a spirit in somebody else's body. We're both just wiped out and need to rest, but we're still here.

"Dad says they're resting," I told Aggie with a frown. "I hope they're okay. I wonder how long they can stay there—in me, I mean. It's not where they're supposed to be, and maybe after a while, they'll..."

Don't panic. I happen to know a spirit can stay inside someone else's body for at least a couple of months, so it's not time to worry about us yet.

How could you possibly know that? I thought incredulously.

Later, Dad said, and I felt him fading to the back of my mind, maybe to rest like he'd said. I hoped so anyway.

Aggie's warm arm wrapped around my shoulders as she rested her head against mine. "Dad's not going out without a fight. And if you think about it, he and Martina have been through a heck of a lot today. Maybe they do need rest. I know I sure do."

She gave a huge yawn, and I couldn't help imitating it.

"Come on," Aggie said, smiling. "It's been a long day, and at least we know we're safe in here. Let's get some sleep. Maybe things will look better in the morning."

I seriously doubted they would, but I nodded and gave her a quick, squeezing hug. "G'night, Aggie."

She kissed her fingers and waggled them at me like she'd always done when we were kids. "Night."

One good thing about the old farmhouse was that it had lots of bedrooms. The family who'd owned it before Grandma and Grandpa had seven kids, and while the rooms were of the pocket-sized variety, it was good that we'd at least all have our privacy. I was sure Bella would be pleased about that arrangement, as she was probably at her limit with both me and my family by now, but I still wanted to check on her before I went to my own little room. After I'd washed my face and plugged in the bathroom nightlight, I headed to her door and gave a quiet knock.

There was silence for so long that I wondered if she'd fallen asleep, but then I heard a soft voice from the other side.

"That you, Howard?"

"It's me," I said.

The door opened a crack, and I was able to slip inside.

By the time I got the door closed behind me, Bella was on her bed with her knees drawn up to her chest. She wore a pair of silky red pajamas Aunt Celia had gotten for me some holiday or birthday, and while they definitely looked better on her than they ever would've on me, the combination of the pj's and the way she was sitting made her look oddly young and vulnerable. I couldn't help giving her a concerned look.

"You okay?"

"None of us are okay." She'd taken her long, dark hair out of its ponytail. It hung loose around her face, blocking her expression from my view. "But hey, at least we finished that damn pie, right?" She gave an unsteady laugh, and I figured it was well past time for an intervention.

I sat on the bed next to her and, thinking of Aggie, put my arm around her shoulders. She tensed at the touch but didn't move away.

"Look," I said. "Belladonna..."

"Just call me Bella," she said with another shaky laugh. "I'm in your grandmother's house wearing your pajamas. My mom is living in your head. I think you can call me Bella."

"But you'll keep calling me Howard?" I asked dryly.

The laugh she gave sounded more real and less unstable than the previous ones. "I don't know. I've been calling you Howard for so long, I'm not sure I could get used to anything else."

"Hey, it's up to you. I mean, I'll be over here kindly and politely doing what you asked and calling you Bella, but if you want to keep calling me Howard, then I guess that's totally fine. Not an insult at all."

To my surprise, she grabbed a pillow from the bed and smacked me with it. "Fine. Alisha." There was a pause. "God, no, it sounds too weird. Like we're—"

"What?"

She looked away. "Like we're friends."

I smiled a little. "Well. Maybe we are."

Bella gave me a horrified look. "God, do you think so?"

"I think we might be," I said solemnly. "I mean, here we are, sitting together on your bed and having a nice heart-to-heart. We spent the whole afternoon together, and you're here staying with me and my family and, as you said, wearing my pajamas. That doesn't sound like the kind of stuff archenemies do."

Bella snorted. "You think of me as your archenemy?"

I felt a spark of annoyance and decided to return the earlier favor by hitting her with a throw pillow. "Yeah, I do. I mean, I did. What did you expect? Ever since I joined the Guardians, you've been trying to take me down in training, humiliate me, or prove you're better than me. I figured you hated me."

Bella was quiet for a moment. "I did...maybe."

"Why though? What did I ever do to you?"

She got to her feet and took a few angry, stalking steps away from the bed. "I don't know. I don't *know*. Maybe it was because everything seemed like it came so easy for you. I had to wait until I was fourteen to join the Guardians, but they let you in at thirteen, and all because your mom was the famous Helen Howard."

"Your mom is head of the *council*," I said incredulously.

She gave a bitter laugh. "You think that did me any favors? I've had to work harder than everybody because Mom wouldn't have a failure as her daughter. I trained and I fought and I worked because I knew the second I failed, the second somebody beat me or I let down my guard, my mom would be right there ready to take me out of the Guardians and send me away to some boarding school in Switzerland or something."

We existed in stunned silence for a moment after that.

"Do you really think she would've done that?"

Bella gave me a dark look. "Why? Is she denying it? Saying she never meant to put so much pressure on me and she would never have sent me away and we're ever so close?"

"No, she's— She and my dad are resting right now. I don't think they can hear us."

Bella sank onto the bed and lay on her back so she could stare up at the ceiling.

"When you were about to join the Guardians, and your mom asked me to look out for you, I was so *angry*. She cared so much about you, and I knew that no matter what happened, she'd always be there for you, no matter how much you screwed up. I was never allowed to screw up. Until today, I guess."

I lay next to her and turned onto my side, propping my head on my hand so I could look at her. "So that's why you were so awful to me? Because you were jealous?"

She gave me an irritated glance. "I mean, not of your clothes or your style or that ugly little bike—"

"Okay," I said.

"But of your family? Yeah. I was. I—I am."

I had the sudden, insane desire to grab Bella and hug her, but instead I put my hand on her arm and squeezed gently.

"I'm sorry things are so bad in your family. But you know, if we make it out of this, and if we decide to keep being friends even when there isn't an apocalypse on the horizon? I'm pretty sure you'll be welcome over at my house anytime. We can— I don't know. We can unofficially adopt you or something. You can become another proud member of the Howard clan. My mom can boss you around, my dad can tell you dopey puns, Jake can drive you crazy with his general Jake-ness, and Aggie can give you that great older sister advice she's so good at."

"And you?" Bella said quietly. She rolled over to face me, and as I looked into her eyes, my heart beat a little faster. This was the closest we'd ever been outside of sparring matches, and the eyes I'd thought were just plain brown were actually dark and deep and ringed with flecks of gold. "What will you do?"

The urge to hug her had transformed confusingly into something else, and I sat up quickly. "I'll be there for you to pick on, I guess." I fought to sound calm and lighthearted and not like I was reevaluating everything in my freaking life. "You can make fun of my clothes and my room and anything else you want. Open season on Alisha."

"You *want* me to make fun of you?"

"Well, no," I said. "But what else would we do together?"

I wanted to call the words back as soon as I'd said them, but instead I squeezed my eyes shut and hoped Bella couldn't see how tense the muscles were in my back and shoulders. There was a long pause, and when I opened my eyes, Bella was right there in front of me, staring into my face with an odd look on hers.

"I can think of a few things," she said quietly.

And then she kissed me.

*

I lay awake in my bed for a long time. Every now and then, my hand would stray to my lips as if questioning the reality of what had happened, and I'd have to force my arm back down to my side and try again to go to sleep. There had been no comment or outcry from Martina or my dad, so I hoped they really were doing the spirit equivalent of sleeping and hadn't witnessed Bella and I making out on her bed because... Well, that was a conversation I was not ready to have. I wasn't even sure I was ready to have it with myself, let alone with my dad and the mother of the girl I'd just kissed.

So instead, I lay there and stared at the ceiling, and the night passed quietly around me. I wondered if Bella was still awake, but thinking about her was dangerous because it made me get all tingly again, and getting tingly over Belladonna was just too freaking weird.

I checked my phone a few times, but there had been no updates from Guardian headquarters. The last message I had was one from Spencer—the night shift version of Lettie—warning all Guardians to stay in their homes and wait for further instructions. Which made some kind of sense, at least. It wasn't like we could fight these things, and it looked like everyone who had tried so far had just been taken over themselves. But while my family was protected by Grandma's barrier, I had to wonder about all the other Guardian families out there and just the people around town in general. How many of them were going to be taken tonight? How would we even know who we could trust when the morning came?

At Mom's insistence, I'd turned off the GPS tracking on my phone. If someone at Guardian HQ had been taken, they could've easily used our phones to figure out exactly where we were, which might be how the vesu had found us. Whatever the case, at least they wouldn't be able to track us now, for whatever good that might do us.

I was still awake around midnight when there was a noise from downstairs.

I sat up in bed, eyes wide and staring into the darkness as I listened.

It had sounded like the front door opening, but that was impossible. No one could get in, and no one should be going out, but I knew what I'd heard. Had Uncle Lucas come home?

I leaped out of bed and hurried out into the hallway, trying to keep quiet out of habit, even though if there really was danger downstairs, waking everyone would've been a much smarter thing to do. The stairs were old and creaky, but I knew just where to step, and I managed to make it down and into the kitchen just in time to see Uncle Lucas step into the glow of the kitchen nightlight.

I stopped dead and stared at him. I was used to him looking tired and drawn, but this was something else altogether. It was like there was a weight on his shoulders, pushing him down. His old tan trench coat was torn in three different places, and I could see a cut on his chin, a bruise on one pale cheek. The eyes that met mine were haunted, but I couldn't tell yet if they really belonged to my Uncle Lucas, or if something else had taken them over.

"Uncle Lucas," I said in a voice that only trembled a little. "What happened?"

He shook his head wordlessly and came forward a few steps, and with a sinking heart, I grabbed Grandma's baseball bat from behind the fridge and brandished it at him.

"Please don't take this personally, but I need to be sure you're really you before I let you in."

The tired look switched to one of surprise, but he stopped where he was and didn't try to come any closer.

"Alisha, I understand your caution, but please know that in my case, it's completely unnecessary."

"I can't be sure of that," I said.

"You can," came a voice from behind me, and I turned to find

Grandma standing in the doorway in the old gray sweatshirt and sweat-pants she wore to bed. "Lucas can't be taken over by those vesu things."

"Why not?" I demanded.

Uncle Lucas gave me a sad, tired smile. "Because I am one of them."

Chapter Eleven

I almost dropped the bat. "*What?* But that's— No! That's insane."

Grandma plucked the bat from my hands and returned it to its place of honor behind the refrigerator. "Let's get a cup of tea brewing, and we can talk this over. Lucas looks about run off his feet."

Grandma headed to the stove to fill the kettle and start it boiling, but I just stared at Uncle Lucas, not understanding and not wanting to understand. I could tell I was hurting him, looking at him like I'd never seen him before, but I couldn't help it. After a moment, he sighed and headed into the dining room to sit down, and I followed numbly after him.

We sat with no sound but the hissing of the water as it heated. My mind spun with questions, but I didn't know how to even begin asking them. A short time later, a steaming cup was set in front of me, another in front of Uncle Lucas, and another at Grandma's place at the head of the table.

"Now," Grandma said after she'd settled herself into her seat, "the first thing you should understand, Alisha, is that this doesn't change a thing about your Uncle Lucas. He's still the same good, kind person he always was. He's my son and your uncle, and nothing's going to change that. Understand?"

"No?" An edge of hysteria crept into my voice.

"Mom, it's okay." Lucas folded his hands on the tabletop and met my gaze, and his eyes looked exactly as they always had, kind and intelligent and full of warmth. "I'll try to explain, and I hope that by the end, maybe you'll be able to understand, at least a little."

I didn't answer because I had no idea what to say, and so Uncle Lucas took a small sip of his tea and began his story.

"I don't have many memories of my earliest days," he said, his blue eyes going soft and distant, "except a sense of darkness and danger pressing in on me from all sides. Living itself was painful, and if I'd existed like that for my entire life, I doubt I could've stayed sane. But as it was, I was lucky. Something happened. I don't know who did it or how it happened, but I was pulled out of that dark place and found myself in a different world. This world. There were blue skies and fresh winds and people, so many people just going about their daily lives, some suffering more and some less, but nearly all of them doing their best to make their little parts of the world better.

"I was fascinated by them, but I didn't know how to talk to them. They couldn't see me, most of them, and it hurt me to go out in the daylight, so I mostly traveled around at night and tried to find someone I could communicate with. Most people didn't notice me, even if I flew right in their houses and hovered around them, but one night I went into a certain house and found a little boy, and he saw me. He reached out his fingers and touched me, and in that moment, it was like something grabbed onto me and pulled. Next thing I knew, I was inside his mind, and I could talk to him and he could talk to me.

"That little boy, Alisha, was your dad. He was only about three at the time, and young enough that the adults around him thought he was talking to an imaginary friend when he started having long conversations with someone he called Lucas. I was just a child myself, really, and it would never have occurred to me to do what others of my kind would have done and push him out of his body so I could take it over. Instead, I just existed there peacefully, and Barry and I became the best of friends.

"But after a while, I started noticing a sadness in him when we talked, and finally he told me that it was because he wished I could come out of his head and be a real boy, someone to play with and spend time with. A friend or a brother. We thought of each other as brothers, even back then, and I started to wish for it too. But there didn't seem to be anything we could do about it, so we talked and played as best we could with me just existing in his mind. But I knew that someday I would have to leave, and that was the last thing I wanted to do.

"And then one day, Barry's father took him to the hospital. His mother had just had a baby, a little brother for Barry, but the birth had been complicated, and things weren't looking particularly good. The baby had been born with the umbilical cord wrapped around his neck, and while they were keeping him on life support for the time being, the doctors were sure he wasn't going to come out of it. Barry's dad tried to explain it to him by saying it was like the baby had a body but no soul, no spirit, and that's when we got the idea."

"So you went into his body?" My voice came out hoarsely and seemed too loud after the softness of Uncle Lucas's voice.

"I did. At first, I wasn't even sure how to do it, but eventually I was able to figure it out. It was the strangest thing I'd ever experienced. One moment, I was floating in the soft darkness of Barry's mind, and then suddenly I was drawing in a breath, and it *hurt*, and there was light and sensation and everything was so loud. The baby made a miraculous recovery, and when Barry insisted that the baby's name was Lucas, Mom and Dad were so happy that they agreed, and that became my name.

"I was born, or created, or spawned, or whatever word you want to use, in a dark place, but there was nothing innately evil about me. I had the chance to live and learn and grow here, with a family that loved me and a brother who supported me, and that's why I am who I am today. If I hadn't, if I'd lived my life in that dark place instead of here, I'd probably be just like the others, twisted and tormented and just wanting to find a way to escape. That's what they want, Alisha. They want to escape the pain they've suffered their entire lives. It doesn't make what they're doing right, but maybe it makes it a little easier to understand."

Uncle Lucas sat back in his chair and let out a soft breath, and I watched him with the weight of all this new, impossible knowledge weighing heavy in my brain.

"When did Grandma find out about all this?"

Grandma had been quietly sipping her tea while Lucas told his story, but now she straightened in her chair. "Oh, he and Barry told me after a while. I didn't believe them when they were kids, but when they got older, I was more inclined to believe. Especially since Lucas here was able to give me a little demonstration by leaving his body and flitting around the room like a damn living shadow for a few minutes. That was pretty convincing."

"I joined the Guardians research team," Uncle Lucas went on, "in hopes of learning more about where I came from, but very little is known about the vesu or their dimension. All we know is that there seems to be an almost endless number of them, and their goal is to break into other dimensions and take over the beings that live there. The good news is that in their bodiless state, they're incapable of opening a gateway between worlds, but unfortunately, they've had no trouble finding other beings willing to do the work for them."

"How do you think you got here?" I asked. "Into our dimension, I mean."

Uncle Lucas frowned. "Honestly, I have no idea. Someone must have opened a rift, and it must have opened exactly where I was in order to pull me through it. Probably an accident. And because no invasion of the vesu followed, I'd guess the rift didn't stay open for long. Unfortunately, the one in the cave has been open for far too long already. Your father closed it, but it looks like they've managed to wrench it back open again."

"Uncle Lucas, what happened tonight? You were going to try to put a barrier up at the cave, but—"

"We failed," he said faintly. He took another sip of his tea, and it seemed to revitalize him a bit. "We got there just before dusk. Still in time, we thought, but they were waiting for us. Our spell casters had barely started the barrier spell when we were attacked."

"But I thought the vesu couldn't come out in the daylight? I know it was almost dusk, but..."

"We were attacked by Grayson and her team, plus Martina and your father. They were too strong for us, and we had to retreat. And by that time, the sun had gone down, and vesu came pouring out of the cave. There were at least a dozen, maybe more. I suspect they used your father's magical knowledge to try to open a gateway to their world, but they weren't able to do so more than a crack. Even using his body, they won't be able to match his magical ability, and that's a very good thing for us. If they'd opened the rift any further, there would've been hundreds or thousands of vesu instead of just a dozen. But they'll keep trying, and they'll keep bringing them through one after another until they have enough to take over our world."

We sat in a dismal silence for a moment.

"So, what can we do?" I asked.

"I have an idea," Uncle Lucas said, "but it's risky."

Another vesu slammed against the barrier outside, making us all jump.

"Honestly, son?" Grandma said. "I think risky is just fine."

*

We got Uncle Lucas settled on the most comfortable couch in the living room, blankets piled around him and pillows to support his back, neck, and head.

"Are you sure about this?" I was kneeling on the carpet beside him, and vesu or not, all I saw when I looked at him was the uncle I'd loved since the first day I'd met him. "This isn't just risky, it's borderline suicidal."

"I'm sure. Your dad and I did some experimenting with this when we were teenagers, so I know I can be away from my body for at least a few hours without any ill effects."

"It'll be light in a few hours," I said. "What if you can't get back before dawn?"

He didn't answer, and impulsively, I leaned forward and wrapped my arms around him. It was an awkward thing to do when he was lying down but a necessary one.

"I love you," I said into his shoulder. "I don't care where you came from or what you used to be. I love you, and I always will."

There was a stunned pause, and then Uncle Lucas's arms came up around me and hugged me back. "I love you too," he said softly. "I hope this isn't my last chance to say so."

I pulled back, aware that my eyes were wet with tears but smiling through them. "It won't be. You be careful, okay? Once you find out what they're planning, you get back here as soon as you can."

Uncle Lucas closed his eyes. His breathing slowed, and his voice was soft when he said, "If I can't get back in time, I'll try to hide out somewhere until I can. Not sure how long I can be away, but I'll try...to get back..."

He sank into what seemed to be a deep sleep. Grandma switched off the lights, and in the pale moonlight from the window, I was able to see a faint, ghostly something rise from his body. It flitted over to me, dancing in front of my face until I couldn't help smiling, then darted over to Grandma and flew great circles around her head.

"All right, enough showing off," she said. "The hole in the barrier will only be open for a second. Get out, do what you have to do, and come back. You know the signal for when you want to get back in."

The ghostly something danced up and down as if nodding. Grandma closed her eyes and made a few quick gestures with her hands, murmuring words I couldn't understand, and I felt a sudden suction as if my ears desperately needed to pop. Uncle Lucas's spirit stole forward and disappeared through the window; then Grandma made an aggressive gesture of closing her fist, and the suction suddenly stopped. I knew the barrier had been closed back up again, with us on one side and Uncle Lucas's spirit on the other.

The only sound in the room was Uncle Lucas's soft breathing.

"Do you think he can do it?" I asked. "Find out what they're planning?"

For the first time, I saw real worry on Grandma's rugged old face. "I sure hope so, sweetheart. I sure hope so."

*

I fought to stay awake, settled down in an old green armchair I'd pulled up next to the couch, but it was too late, and I was too exhausted. I drifted off after about half an hour, and when I snapped awake sometime later, the world outside the window was gray instead of black, and I knew it was nearly dawn.

I sat up straight, pushed off the afghans Grandma had draped over me, and got to my feet. Uncle Lucas lay still and apparently sleeping on the couch, and I knew with a sinking certainty that he hadn't made it back yet. He was still out there somewhere, floating around free and unprotected in a sea of malevolent creatures, and there was nothing we could do to help him get back.

Grandma was still in the same spot as when I'd fallen asleep, sitting in her favorite rocking chair and sewing a patch onto a ripped pair of pants. Her hand was steady, drawing the needle in and out of the fabric with easy confidence, and I wondered how she could be so calm when both her sons had been separated from their bodies.

"Work keeps us grounded." Grandma didn't look up from her sewing. "The worse you feel, the better it is to go do some work. If it doesn't make you feel better, then at least you got something productive done while you were feeling awful."

I could see the wisdom in that, but at the same time, I kind of wanted to knock the sewing out of her hands and demand she feel as terrified as I did. Instead, I turned my attention to Uncle Lucas. His body anyway. A press of his wrist showed that his pulse was steady and strong, and his breathing seemed fine too. He did seem to just be sleeping, except that everything that made him *him* had left. It gave me a strange, dizzy feeling to think about, so I tried not to. But for the first time, it occurred to me that before this was all over, I could be booted out of my body just like Dad and Martina had been, and the thought of being me but no longer in my body made me want to run off screaming.

Instead, I got up to make a cup of tea, because I was sure that was the first thing Uncle Lucas would want when he came back. And he *was* going to come back, I'd decided. He was, because I couldn't imagine living in a world that didn't have him in it, so that left him no choice but to come back.

Grandma didn't have a large tea selection, but I found an ancient oolong teabag at the bottom of the tea tin and dropped it into a cup while the water boiled. The kettle was just starting to whistle when I heard a *thump* from the living room, and I just had the presence of mind to switch off the stove before I went dashing back.

Grandma had dropped her sewing and stood there rigidly, staring at the window. Dawn was breaking—I could clearly make out the shadows of the trees and the barn, now, and there was a faint pinkness to the far-off horizon—and I knew that if Uncle Lucas was going to come back, it was going to have to be now.

"That was one," Grandma said. "Come on, Lucas. *Come on.*"

The first thump was followed by two more, then a pause, then three in quick succession, then a pause and one more, and Grandma gave a little cry and swept her hands into the gesture I'd seen her do earlier. A tiny hole in the barrier opened with the previous suction, and a ghostly shadow flitted through, flew across the room, and disappeared into Uncle Lucas's chest.

Grandma gasped a few more words to seal the barrier as she ran to Lucas's side, and then we both were kneeling by the couch, staring down into Uncle Lucas's face with hope and worry and fear. How sure were we that the shadow that had come in was Uncle Lucas? What if it was some other creature that had gotten the code out of him and come here to take us down from the inside?

Uncle Lucas's eyelids fluttered, and then his eyes slid open and gazed at us. He looked weak and disoriented, and when Grandma put a restraining hand on his chest, he didn't struggle against it.

"What did you and your brother give me on Mother's Day after your grandmother died?" Grandma demanded.

Lucas blinked at her a few times, then coughed and said hoarsely, "Flowers we picked from Mrs. McCarthy's garden."

"Which ones?"

"The lilies. The ones she'd been growing for that contest."

"And what did I do when I found out you'd stolen those flowers?"

Uncle Lucas gave a faint smile. "You hugged us and said Mrs. McCarthy deserved to lose that contest for once in her life."

Grandma lifted her hand from Lucas's chest. "She beat me every year, but not that one. I never could convince her I hadn't sent you boys over there to sabotage her on purpose." She leaned down and kissed Uncle Lucas gently on the forehead. "Welcome back, sweetheart. What did you find out?"

"Help me sit up," he said, and Grandma and I worked together to ease him into a sitting position. He put a hand to his head and looked a little dizzy, and it was then I remembered the tea. By the time I got back with it, Uncle Lucas seemed a bit steadier, and he took the teacup gratefully.

"It won't have had time to brew yet," I said, but he shook his head and took a sip anyway.

"My mouth feels like cotton. I've never been away for this long before." He shuddered and took another sip. "I don't recommend it."

We waited impatiently as he took another few drinks; then he handed the cup to me and took a deep breath.

"I know what they're planning," he said. "And I think I might know how to stop them."

Chapter Twelve

We had our council of war around the breakfast table. Mom, Aggie, Jake, Bella, Grandma, Uncle Lucas, and I feasted on pancakes, tofu scramble, and fruit while we discussed how we were going to stop the world from ending.

"The council has called an emergency meeting," Uncle Lucas said, and I was pleased to see he was looking much heartier and healthier after a few pancakes and a strong cup of black tea. "It's going to happen today at Guardian headquarters, and from the intelligence we've gathered—" Grandma and I pointedly did not look at each other as he said this. "—the vesu are going to infiltrate it. During the night, they managed to get to a number of Guardians and even a few council members, and when the meeting is in full swing, they're going to release the bodiless vesu into the room and take over as many of the Guardians as they can. With the local Guardians taken, no one will be able to stand against them. They'll be able to use the Guardian spell casters to open a steady gateway between our world and theirs, and the invasion will begin."

"So, what do we do?" Jake asked. "How do we stop them?"

"We'll need two teams to get this done. One will go to the cave to take control of the dimensional weak spot and seal up the rift, and the other will go to Guardian headquarters to take out the vesu before they can attack."

"How do we do that?" Belladonna asked. "How do we take them out?"

"There's a spell," Uncle Lucas said. "It's an old one and very difficult to cast, but if we can manage it when everyone is together at headquarters, we should be able to draw the vesu out of the bodies they've stolen and capture them. By that time, hopefully, our second team will have managed to get control of the cave, and we'll be able to send the vesu back to their own dimension before we seal up the rift for good."

"What about everyone else?" Aggie said. "What about the people who got taken by the vesu but aren't at Guardian headquarters?"

There was a short silence, our previous high spirits deflating.

"I wish we could help them all." The pain was clear in Uncle Lucas's soft voice. "But the most important thing now is to clear the Guardians of vesu and get the rift sealed up. After that, we can try to help anyone else who was taken."

Sounds like a good plan, came a voice from inside my head, and I jumped in my seat.

"Dad!"

All eyes turned to me, and I settled back down with an embarrassed look. "Sorry, just...Dad's back. He says it sounds like a good plan."

"Is my mom there too?" Bella's tone was casual, but I knew from the way she kept her eyes fixed on her plate that she felt anything but.

Martina? I thought.

I'm here, came Martina's voice.

Are you okay? Both of you, I mean.

Sleeping without a body is quite a disconcerting experience, but I do at least feel more rested than before.

Me too, kiddo. I feel all rested up and ready to fight some monsters and get my body back.

"She's there," I told Bella. "Both of them slept, I guess, and they're feeling better. They want to help us."

Uncle Lucas gave me a thoughtful look. "I do think they can help. The problem is, though, that we need Barry in one place and Martina in the other."

I frowned at him. "What do you mean?"

"Your father knows how to seal the dimensional wall, so we need him at the cave. But Martina knows everything about Guardian Headquarters and the council, so we need her there. Which means we have to get one of them out of you and into someone else's body."

My eyes widened, and I felt surprise radiating from the two spirits inside me.

Is that even possible? asked Martina.

"Martina wants to know if that's even possible," I said. "And, yeah, I'd kind of like to know too."

"It should be possible. I can walk you through it."

"So who goes, and where do they go?" Mom asked. She'd been oddly quiet up until now, but I could see her looking at the available options around the table and not particularly liking any of them.

"I was thinking Martina's spirit could go into you," Uncle Lucas said, and I at least prepared for an explosion. Mom had never made a secret of how she disliked Martina, and having to share a mind with her? Uh-uh.

But Mom, though her eyes widened a bit at first, nevertheless gave a curt nod and said, "I suppose that's the only choice that makes sense."

"So what are me and Aggie going to do?" Jake asked.

"We need someone to stay behind and get the word out if things go wrong," Uncle Lucas said, a highly diplomatic way of telling my siblings they had to stay home while the rest of us went off to fight. "We can't keep in contact through the earpieces because the vesu have them too, and they'll be able to monitor our communications. But we can keep in touch by text, and if we fail today, it'll be your job to contact the Guardians in other cities and tell them what happened."

Aggie shot me an anxious look but nodded, and although I knew Jake wouldn't be happy to be left behind, he had to know it was better this way.

"Wait," Jake said. "So the Guardians in other cities—they're not coming to help?"

"They've been instructed to stay away for the time being, for their own safety. If the vesu can't be contained by nightfall tonight, a barrier is going to be put up around the city to contain the situation. It's a last resort, and it will essentially doom anyone still in town, but it will at least prevent the vesu from spreading while the world council figures out how to stop them."

"So no pressure, then," I said.

Uncle Lucas gave me a grim smile. "Alisha, Belladonna, do you feel up to heading back to that cave?"

Bella and I exchanged glances, the first real interaction we'd had since the night before. I'd thought it would be awkward, meeting her eyes when the last thing we'd done was kiss, but somehow it wasn't. Looking into her eyes felt like the most natural thing in the world. I couldn't help smiling, and she smiled back.

"We absolutely do," I said.

"Good. You two will need to get past whatever security the vesu have set up and get to the tear in the dimensional wall. Hopefully, we'll be able to capture the vesu at headquarters and get them to the cave by then, but if we don't, don't wait for us. Get your dad's help to seal up the rift, and we'll deal with the captured vesu some other way."

"Not that I doubt you, Uncle Lucas," I said, "but getting all those vesu captured sounds like some serious magic. How are you and Mom going to get a spell like that cast?"

"As it happens," Uncle Lucas said, looking over at Grandma, "we have a secret weapon."

Grandma's face was stern. "You know how I feel about the Guardians, Lucas."

"And I know how you feel about your family, and protecting them and this world." He reached across the table to grip her hand. "Mom, you're the most powerful spell caster we have. We need you for any of this to work."

Grandma didn't look pleased, but finally she gave a curt nod.

Moving Martina from my mind to Mom's ended up being unexpectedly simple. Mom and I sat facing each other on comfortable chairs in the living room while Uncle Lucas stood to one side of us and Grandma stood on the other.

"Can Martina hear me?" Uncle Lucas asked.

"She can hear you," I said.

"Martina, I need you to focus on what separates you from what's around you. Focus on what is *you*, not Alisha, in Alisha's mind. When you've done that, try moving that part of you. Move yourself forward until you can see a light."

And go toward the light? Dad said in a dry voice.

"Dad, shh," I said.

"Poltergeist joke?" Uncle Lucas said wearily.

"Dad loves his eighties movies."

Mom rolled her eyes, and Grandma said, "Barry, focus," in a stern voice.

"After you've found the light, go to it and you'll find yourself outside of Alisha's body. All you'll need to do, then, is find your way into Helen's and enter her mind just as you did Alisha's yesterday."

All right, I'm going to try this, Martina said. *If this doesn't work, Alisha, I hope— I hope you'll tell Bella how much I've regretted everything that's happened between us. And please tell her I would never have sent her away. She's my daughter, and while I'm not good at saying it, I'm proud of her. Tell her that, and also... I hope you'll take care of her.*

I looked nervously toward Bella, who was sitting on the couch nearby watching the proceedings tensely, and elected not to reply.

"Okay," I said. "She's going to try it."

Tension spread through the group, and I wondered if I would feel anything during all of this—if I would feel Martina go if she went. A few seconds passed, and then more, with nothing happening.

Come on, Tina, you can do it! Dad said.

I'm trying! came Martina's irritated voice. *It's a little more difficult than it looks.*

Here, maybe I can give you a push...

Don't you dare!

Whether it was Dad's push or Martina figuring things out on her own, something worked, because I had a sudden sensation of coolness in my forehead and a small white wisp popped out into the air in front of me.

Bella's voice was a hoarse whisper. "Mom?"

The wisp hovered there for a moment, and then it zipped forward to my mom, stopped in front of her as if hesitating, and vanished into her head.

Mom closed her eyes. Her jaw was tight, and there was a deep frown line in her forehead.

Did it work? Dad asked anxiously. *Did she make it?*

The silence seemed to last forever, and then Mom opened her eyes. "She did it," Mom said. "She's here."

Bella collapsed onto the couch in relief, and the tension of the room suddenly relaxed.

Thank God for that, Dad said. *But I have to say, I'll kind of miss having her in here with me. She sure made things more interesting.*

And I'm sure she'll make things real *interesting for Mom,* I thought back, and Dad laughed.

We all got to our feet, and I opened my mouth to ask if Bella and I should get suited up—

"Jake! Alisha!"

Everyone froze as a voice called from outside, one I would've known anywhere. Jake and I exchanged incredulous looks.

"Guinevere?" he said.

We ran to the front door. The barrier extended over the front porch, so Jake and I were able to go outside and stare out into the front yard.

It was Gwen. She stood in the yard wearing a soft cotton nightshirt and leggings with a pair of boots that were only half laced. Her hair was a mess, hanging in purple tangles that clung to the sides of her face, and she wasn't wearing any makeup, the first time she'd gone outside without it in all the time I'd known her.

"Gwen!" I shouted. "How did you get here?"

"Please, you have to let me in." Her eyes were wild with fear, and the look of pain and terror on her face wrenched at my heart and almost propelled me forward into the barrier. "My dad— Something's wrong with him. It's like something took him over. He tried to get me to go with him somewhere, but it was like he was some other person, so I ran. I got a ride from a farmer, and she dropped me off here. I didn't know where else to go." She stopped at the edge of the barrier and held her hands up to it. The magic sizzled against her touch. "Please, you have to let me in. I think someone's following me. If you don't let me in, I don't know what they might do."

"Grandma, take it down!" I'd never heard Jake so upset before. "Let her in, before they get her too!"

Grandma came to stand beside us on the porch, and she and I exchanged glances. She gave me a tight nod, and I turned to Gwen with hope but not much of it.

"Guinevere," I said, "before we let you in, I have to ask you something."

"*Now?*" She glanced back over her shoulder nervously. "Can't you ask me after I'm inside? Please, Alisha, I'm so scared."

Another wrench of my heart, but I swallowed through a dry throat and said, "It'll only take a second. We just have to make sure you're really you."

"Of course, I'm really me! What are you talking about?" She gave another nervous glance behind her and then turned back with new determination in her eyes. "Look, I can prove that I'm me. I can tell you something from a long time ago, something only I would know."

The dread grew inside me, but I still said, "Okay. What is it?"

"When we were twelve, we had a sleepover. I was so nervous

because I'd finally decided to tell you about me. About Jordan."

My eyes widened, and I could feel the confusion radiating from Jake beside me.

"Who's Jordan?" he asked.

"I showed you a picture of a little boy in red swim trunks. It was Jordan. It was me."

Jake's mouth dropped open, but I barely noticed, my heart sinking as I looked out at Gwen. Or whatever had taken Gwen.

I turned back to Grandma and mouthed, "Vesu."

Grandma acknowledged this with a fractional tilt of her head and fixed her eyes on Gwen. "All right, honey, we'll let you in." To my surprise, she strode to the edge of the porch and opened a hole in the barrier large enough for Gwen to come through.

Gwen hurried inside, the barrier closed behind her—and Grandma snapped out a spell that surrounded Gwen in blue light.

"Hey!" Gwen's fists hammered against the new, smaller barrier that encased her like a shimmering cage. "What are you *doing*?"

I stared at the face of my best friend now twisted up in rage. I think I'd known all along, but Gwen, who had been so scared for Jake to find out she was trans, who had only told me after she was absolutely sure she could trust me, would never have talked so openly about her past—not to mention said her deadname, which still made her flinch when she heard it—in front of both Jake and my grandma. But then how had the vesu known?

Suddenly, it hit me. What did Gwen do every single night, even when a friend was sleeping over and would've appreciated her attention? "Her diary," I said. I fixed my gaze on the dark eyes that held nothing of my friend in them. "You read it, didn't you? You read her diary, so we'd think you were her."

Not-Gwen hissed, which was startling enough, even with the barrier up, for me to jump back a step. "She was reading it when we got her," Not-Gwen snarled. "Thinking about how she was going to tell her sweet new boyfriend her secret. And wasn't it nice that he'd told her exactly where all of you were hiding?"

There was a look of pure rage on Jake's face. "You get out of her!" he yelled. "Get out of Gwen!"

"Easy, now," Grandma said. "As it happens, this gives us a perfect opportunity to test something out."

Not-Gwen hissed again, and I eyed the barrier around her nervously. "What do you mean?"

Grandma gave a tight smile. "Now's our chance to test if we can kick one of these bastards out of a body they've taken over."

Not-Gwen screamed and threw herself against the barrier, but Grandma just twitched her finger and the glowing blue cage followed us into the house, giving Not-Gwen no choice but to stumble along with it. Mom, Aggie, Bella, and Uncle Lucas had hung back in the pantry, but they'd clearly heard everything that had been said. Uncle Lucas had his hand held out—palm outward—at Not-Gwen, and Mom and Bella were both holding weapons, Mom with her longsword and Bella with Grandma's refrigerator bat.

"You can put your weapons away," Grandma said mildly. "There won't be a need for them, and even if there was, you're not stabbing holes into this poor girl's body just because some nasty creature's taken it over. Lucas, get my old books out of the attic, will you?"

*

Grandma and Uncle Lucas got set up in the big bedroom upstairs, pushing all the furniture to one side and positioning Not-Gwen in her shimmery cage in the center of the floor. As Uncle Lucas ushered the rest of us out, saying things about concentration, quiet, and a total lack of distractions, Grandma was drawing a big circle on the floor around Not-Gwen with what looked like a stick of charcoal.

"Wait downstairs," Uncle Lucas said as he closed the door firmly but kindly in our faces. "If something goes wrong, you'll know it."

Everyone filed down the stairs, but Jake stayed behind, his hand pressed to the closed door. I lingered in the hallway behind him, not sure what to say or if there even was anything I could say.

He didn't look at me when he said, "Was that really true, what Gwen— What that thing said? Gwen used to be a guy?"

"Gwen was always a girl," I said quietly. "No matter what people called her back then, she's always been Gwen."

Jake didn't answer, and I watched him with more than a little apprehension. I genuinely wasn't sure how he was going to handle this. I mean, both of his sisters liked girls, and he'd never had a problem with it, but guys were weird sometimes about things like this.

Just when I was ready to grab him by the shoulders and shake him and scream that Gwen had always been Gwen, and there was no reason to get freaked out, his tense shoulders relaxed a bit, and he took a step away from the door.

"That must've been really tough for her. Knowing she was a girl but having everybody around her say she wasn't." He took a few more steps, as if thinking things through. "And now she's happy, living the life that feels right to her, and some asshole from another dimension wants to steal that away from her? That's not fair, is it? That's not fair!"

The bedroom door opened, and Grandma stood there with a wrathful look on her face. "Jakey, I can see you're mighty upset about your girlfriend, but would you mind going downstairs so we might actually have a shot at getting her body back for her?"

Jake ducked his head meekly. "Yes, Grandma. Sorry, Grandma. We're going."

Grandma gave him a stern nod, but when her eye caught mine, her lips twitched upward. Then she closed the door and went back to the business of trying to save my best friend.

As we started down the stairs, Jake glanced at me in apprehension. "Even if they get that thing out of her, how are they going to get Gwen back into her body? We don't even know where she is, or if—if she's okay."

"She must still be in her house," I said, though my stomach twisted at the thought. "We'll just go and get her spirit and put it back in her body."

"Should we go right now?" Jake said. "We should go right now, right? So it's ready for her when they get that thing out of her body. How are we going to carry it? You think I could put it in my bookbag or my pocket or—or—like, a jar or something—"

"Easy, there," I said. "We'll see what Grandma says. Anyway, the barrier's still up around the house, so we couldn't go now even if we wanted to. For now, all we can do is wait."

He looked crestfallen, but some of the old Jake stubbornness managed to poke through. "I'm not good at waiting."

I patted him on the shoulder. "None of us are, little brother, so it should be a fun time all around."

Chapter Thirteen

"I don't know about you," Belladonna said, "but I never thought the end of the world would involve so much sitting around."

The two of us sat together on the back porch swing, staring out into my grandmother's backyard. The air was warm and smelled sweet, fresh, and earthy, and the sun was high enough in the sky to flood the fields with gold. Bella and I sat close but not close enough to touch, and our feet moved in unison to push the swing gently back and forth, back and forth. It was really nice.

Still...

Dad, I hope you don't take this the wrong way, but could you possibly give Bella and me some privacy?

There was a pause. *I guess you want to talk to her about that smooch from last night, huh?*

I felt my cheeks heating up and hoped Bella wouldn't notice. *Oh, no, Dad, you didn't— You didn't see that, did you?*

Just a glimpse. I was asleep, or whatever the soul-trapped-in-another-body equivalent of it is, but I still got some little flashes of what was going on. Seems like you've changed your mind about Bella a tiny bit, huh?

A tiny bit, I thought, still fighting general mortification at being caught making out by the disembodied spirit of my father. *She's been through a lot, and I think that's made it hard for her to be with people, or to trust them. Anyway, I just need to talk to her about some stuff, and if there's any way you could...*

Sure, kiddo, I get it. No offense taken. Guess I'll head back to that cozy back part of your mind and try to take another nap. Probably a good idea to be as rested as possible for what we have to do today anyway.

I smiled softly. *Thanks, Dad. I love you, you know.*

I love you too. See you in a bit.

Because I was paying attention to it this time, I actually felt his consciousness withdraw, and it left me with a lonely, empty feeling I didn't want to think about too deeply. Dad would come out of this okay. He *would*.

Pushing away this latest in a veritable Mount Everest of worries, I turned to Belladonna.

"Bella, I—I kind of want to talk. About what happened last night, I mean."

Bella had been gazing out at the golden fields with a faint smile on her face, but now the smile faded and her jaw tightened. "Okay," she said in a wary voice. "What about it?"

"It was great," I said, and it was important that I turn away from her at that moment because I could feel myself getting all warm and tingly again and did not want it to distract me. "It was more than great. But

I guess I'm just wondering why you did it. Why you kissed me. Did it mean something, or was it just a spur of the moment thing and now we're back to being how we were before, or what? I know this is a weird time to be talking about this, but we really might die today, and I figure if I want answers, now's the time to get them."

I didn't have much experience with romance, but I was fairly sure this wasn't what you were supposed to say after exchanging a lip-lock with someone you'd thought you'd hated for years. But then, I'd never been one for doing things the right way, had I?

Bella didn't say anything for a while.

"Look," she said, "if you want to know the truth..."

"That's kind of what I'm looking for, yeah."

"The truth is, I kissed you because— I just wanted to, okay? I saw you there and I wanted to kiss you, so I did. It doesn't have to mean anything if you don't want it to."

"What if I do want it to?'

Bella's eyes widened. There was something quietly vulnerable in her voice when she said, "You do?"

I nodded.

It seemed like we might be about to fall into each other's arms while the music swelled, but then Bella turned away. Her hair slid over her face like a curtain. "You don't mean that."

"Um. Excuse me?"

"You don't mean it," Bella said. "I mean, come on. The whole damn world might be ending. Everything's completely crazy. Sure, maybe you think you mean it now, but what happens when things go back to normal? *If* they go back to normal? Are you seriously telling me you're ready to walk into school on Monday with me as your—as whatever this is?"

Anger rose in me, and I glared at her. "Okay, look, I might not be the most experienced when it comes to things like this, but I'm pretty sure you don't get to decide how I'm feeling. You want to know how I feel? How I feel right now? Don't answer that," I cut in before she could speak, "because I'm going to tell you anyway."

I hesitated, then took her hand in mine and held it tightly.

"I'm scared," I said. "I'm terrified. My best friend is upstairs right now with a monster inside her, and I don't know if we'll ever be able to get her back. And that might happen to all of us, and that's the scariest thing I've ever faced in my life. But you know what else I feel? When I look at you, I feel like there's someone there I want to know. I feel like I never really saw you before, but now all I see is you. I stayed up half the night last night thinking about you kissing me, and I woke up this morning thinking about the same thing. And believe me, there are lots of other things I could have been thinking about. So don't tell me I don't mean it, or I won't feel this way if things go back to normal. This is how I feel, and if you don't feel the same way, that's fine, but don't tell me I'm not allowed to like you, because I do."

I sat back against the swing and had to take a few deep breaths.

Bella's hand was warm in mine, and I felt her give my fingers a quick, tentative squeeze.

"You're so freaking dramatic," she said.

"Not news, believe me."

Her thumb stroked the back of my hand, and I risked meeting her eyes.

"I'm not good at this," she said quietly. "I don't date people. I don't even think I have friends, really. So I hope you know that there's a really good chance I could screw this up. Like, a lot."

I snorted. "You think I have a clue what I'm doing either? This is the first time for me too, and I don't know, I think I'm kind of excited to see how it'll go." I smiled at her. "So, what do you say? Kiss me while the world is ending?"

She squeezed my hand and leaned in, and we both forgot our troubles for a while.

*

About an hour had passed before Grandma came downstairs. We were all sitting listlessly in the living room, not speaking or doing much of anything, but we stared at her as she made her way down the stairs and stared some more when she came to a stop at the bottom.

"Alisha," she said. "We need you up there."

I swallowed. Grandma's expression was solemn, giving away nothing, so after a glance at Jake's fearful face, I got up and followed her to the second floor. I wasn't sure what I expected as she ushered me into the big bedroom, but it wasn't to see Gwen sitting calmly on the floor, still surrounded by blue light but looking more like herself than she had before.

Her face lit up when she saw me. "Alisha! I'm so glad to see you."

"What's going on?" I said in a low voice to Grandma.

Uncle Lucas, who I now saw had been sitting in a chair in the corner, got to his feet to answer me. "We think we've got her back, but we need to be sure."

"Got her back? Really? How?"

Grandma smiled a little, and I noticed for the first time that she looked tired. "It wasn't easy, but after we got that thing out of her, we tried summoning her spirit, to see if we could get it to come back on its own."

"But it's daylight," I said. "How could it—"

"That was the tricky part," Grandma said. "We had to open a portal, which is a damn tricky thing to do under any circumstances, so the soul could get to us. I have to tell you, it was pretty shaky there for a while, but I think it worked."

I looked back at Gwen, who sat in a ray of sunlight from the window feeling her fingers and hands as if she couldn't believe she was touching them. It sure seemed like Gwen, but I didn't dare believe it until I was sure.

"What happened to the vesu?" I asked.

Uncle Lucas gestured to a sturdy wooden box sitting on the dresser. Its padlock glowed faintly. "Contained."

I bit my lip and, after an encouraging glance from Grandma, went to sit by Gwen on the carpet, as close as I could get to her with the barrier still in place.

"Gwen?" I said. "Is that really you?"

She smiled her biggest, fullest smile, and a soft flutter of hope kindled in my chest.

"It's really me," she said in her soft, husky voice. "Hard to believe when I look like such a mess, but it's me."

My eyes brimmed with tears, but I wiped them away. "Look, I hope you don't think this is weird, but I need to ask you some questions. Really specific ones, to make sure you're you."

She laughed. "Nothing could be weirder than whatever just happened to me. Go ahead and ask. I'll try to answer, though my brain feels like it just got run through a dishwasher or something."

"Okay," I said, and every fiber of my being was united in a chorus of *Please, please, please, please, please.* "Back when we first met. You'd just moved to town, and Jake and I went riding by your house on our bikes. What was the first thing you said to me?"

She grinned. "I said your eye shadow was fierce."

"And?"

"And that your brother was cute."

"And he was, back then," I said. It was Gwen. I was almost positive it was Gwen, but she might've written about our first meeting in her diary, so I knew I had to find something else, something she would never have written down. "Okay, I have one more question."

"I'm ready."

"I told you something once. I made you promise never to tell anyone, and never to even write it down in case someone could read it. What was it?"

There was a silence, and my hopeful feelings started to sink.

But then Gwen locked eyes with me and said, so quietly that I doubted if Grandma or Uncle Lucas could hear her, "You told me that you were afraid to grow up and get boobs, because you thought Jake wouldn't want to play with you anymore if you did."

Boy, did I pick the wrong moment to come back, Dad said.

Tears filled my eyes and I laughed out loud. "Take it down," I told Grandma. "Take the barrier down. It's her. It's really her."

Grandma made a gesture and the blue light vanished, and I threw myself at Gwen and hugged her hard.

"I'm so glad you're you," I said, squeezing her tight.

She hugged me back just as tightly. "Me too. Believe me."

When Jake came up, his expression soft and hopeful, I backed out of the room to give him and Gwen their privacy. But I couldn't help noticing that the first thing he did was wrap his arms around Gwen and kiss her, and I knew that if we all survived this, Gwen and Jake were going to be all right.

Chapter Fourteen

An hour later, we were suited up and ready to go. I stepped out into the morning sunlight with my armor a snug, comforting weight against me, and it felt good to have the sun on my face and know that none of the vesu could come near us now that it was daylight.

None of the ones without bodies anyway, Dad pointed out.

Can you just let me enjoy this one moment of safety, Dad?

A thousand pardons, my dear.

Bella and I tossed our standard duffel bags full of weapons and gear into the trunk of her convertible, and it was weird to think of all that had changed between us since the last time we'd had occasion to store these things there.

There was lots of tearful hugging with Jake, Aggie, and Gwen, and Grandma made sure they knew exactly where the leftovers were in the fridge in case they got hungry while waiting to find out if we were all doomed or not. I gave all three of them some pretty bone-crushing hugs myself, but I couldn't bring myself to say any words like "goodbye," so instead I just squeezed them quietly and then headed to the car with Bella.

This won't be goodbye, Dad said. *Not if I have anything to do with it.*

Damn straight, I said.

Now, where in hell did you learn that kind of language? Dad said, and I grinned.

"I have to say, I'll be glad when your dad's back in his own body," Bella said as she slid into the driver's seat beside me. "At least then I won't have to wonder what you're smiling about all the time."

"I guess you'll just have to give me other reasons to smile," I said, which even I had to admit was really nauseatingly sappy.

Bella, to her credit, made a disgusted face before grinning and kissing me. "Ready to do this?"

"Not a bit," I said. "But what the hell, let's do it anyway."

*

We held hands over the gearshift as we drove, and the morning was warm and sunny and fragrant with a strange combination of summery sweetness and the sharper, crisper scent of the coming autumn. It was like the seasons were balanced somewhere between life and death, and I hoped it wasn't Mother Nature giving us a dark hint about how our day was going to go.

We were about a mile away from the riverside trail when Bella swore.

"What?" I said.

"There's a cop behind us."

Instead of twisting around and gaping, I directed my gaze to the side mirror and saw that there was, indeed, a police cruiser cruising along just behind us.

"So? His lights aren't—"

Bella's fingers tightened on the wheel as blue light flickered from behind us. "You were saying?"

"Crap," I said. "But, I mean, you weren't speeding, were you?"

"No, but perhaps you will recall that we have an arsenal of weapons in our trunk, and we're wearing freaking *armor*?"

"Ah."

A siren gave a quick, cut-off wail from behind us, and a gloved hand reached out of the cruiser's driver's side window and motioned us to pull over. Bella saw it too, and there was a moment when I was sure she was going to stamp her foot on the gas and try to outrun him. But in the end, she pulled over to the side of the road and sat there seething with her arms folded.

"This is all we need," she muttered.

"Easy," I said. "It'll be fine. We're just two innocent, armor-wearing girls heading out for a morning hike."

"Right."

The officer came around to Bella's side of the car. It wasn't a "him" at all, but a tall, sturdy-looking blonde woman with her hair in a low ponytail and an oversized pair of sunglasses covering her eyes.

Bella, perhaps reading from the script of *Things People Say When Stopped By Police*, squinted up at the woman and said, "Is there a problem, Officer?"

A name badge on the officer's black uniform read, "SHELBY."

Shelby gave us a long look through her sunglasses. "Where are you girls headed?"

I glanced down at my thick cloth armor, but Bella answered without blinking, "The gym."

Shelby's expression didn't change. "Would you step out of the car, please?"

My veins filled with ice, and all I could do was stare uncomprehendingly.

"Officer, with all due respect," Bella said carefully, "I think we have a right to know if we did something wrong."

"With all due respect," Shelby said, "I think you have the right to listen to what I tell you and step out of the car."

My eyes were suddenly locked onto the gun at her hip, and while she hadn't made any moves to draw it, all the stories I'd ever heard about situations like this came flooding back to me, and I was suddenly scared. Really, truly scared. I was more afraid of this blonde woman with a badge and a gun than I was of an invasion of body-stealing shadow monsters, and that was pretty messed up.

"All right," I said in placating tones. "We'll get out."

Keeping my arms out, hands up and fingers spread, I opened the passenger side door and stepped out onto the side of the road. Bella glared bloody murder at Officer Shelby, but she got out too, and a moment later Shelby was poking around inside the car, opening the glove compartment and even peeking under the seat.

"Would you open the trunk for me, please?"

Bella paled, and I wondered what we could possibly do to get out of this. Everyone was counting on us to get to that cave and seal up the dimensional tear—we couldn't exactly afford to get carted off to jail. And who would even get us out?

Bella straightened, however, and leveled a calm look on Officer Shelby. "Sorry, the lock's been broken for about a month now. There's nothing in there but a spare tire and some junk anyway."

Shelby stared at her so silently and for so long that I felt cold sweat start to trickle down my back. Finally, Shelby gave a tight nod and headed back to her cruiser. Bella and I gaped at each other, wondering if we were truly going to be let off—and then Shelby was back with a crowbar.

"Lucky for us I've got a key that'll open any lock." Before either of us could react, she wedged the crowbar into a gap in the trunk and pushed down hard. The trunk popped obligingly open.

"Well, well, well," Shelby said, now apparently reading from the script of *Things Police Say When Finding Something Incriminating.* "No spare tire in sight, but I wonder what's in these bags?"

"Run," Bella whispered to me. "We have to run."

Shelby was bent over the contents of the trunk, so her eyes weren't on us at that moment, but I still hesitated. Run? To *where*? But we couldn't be caught here. We couldn't. But if we ran, we'd be leaving most of our weapons behind, which was kind of counterproductive to what we were trying to do here. And did we really want to get in serious, genuine trouble with the law? But what did it matter if the world ended today?

Alisha, she's right. You have to run. Now.

Dad's words broke me out of my confused thoughts, and I grabbed Bella's hand. We ran.

Shelby shouted something after us, but of course we ignored her, leaving the road, vaulting over a farmer's fence, and starting a mad dash across a field. There were some woods in the distance, and if we could just make it there—

The officer shouted again, and they were no words I'd ever heard before, though there was something familiar about the rhythm and tone.

She's casting a spell, Dad said urgently. *Get down. Get down right now.*

"Bella, get down!" I screamed as I hurled myself to the ground.

A stinging, searing heat surged by just over my head, and I squinted up into a stream of actual fire. I lay in the grass and the dirt for a full five seconds after the fire stream ended, breathing hard and trying to process what had just happened. To my relief, I could hear Bella swearing fervently a few feet away, sounding shocked and angry rather than injured. I got to my feet and stared back at the road.

Officer Shelby stood by the fence, her hand still outstretched from the fire spell that had nearly burned both Bella and me to cinders. The air smelled like smoke and ashes, and Shelby had taken her sunglasses off and was staring at us with a strange, twisted smile on her face.

Vesu. She was a vesu. And she didn't want to take us over. She wanted to kill us. And because neither Bella nor I could do any magic at all, she would succeed.

Dad, I thought desperately, *I can't do magic, but you can. Use me. Do magic through me. That's the only way we're going to get out of this.*

"Howard, what do we do?" Bella said shakily.

"Hold on, I'm on it."

"How are you on it!?"

Dad's determination was a growing warmth in my mind. *I don't know if I can, but I'll sure as hell try. But I think— I think you need to do something. I think you need to give me control.*

I had no idea how to do that, and I could tell that Not-Shelby was ramping up for another attack, but I still squeezed my eyes shut and focused. *I give you control. I give you control. I give my dad control.*

I just kept repeating it, trying to visualize what might be going on inside me, trying to picture my dad's ghostly spirit spreading through my body and taking over control of my limbs, my mouth, my voice—

It was like sinking. One moment I was there, me, in full control of myself and my body, and the next I was submerged in a dark, warm space that cradled me like a child, holding me close, keeping me safe and hidden. I was dimly aware that I was still in my body and that things were happening outside, but it was hard to care when I floated in the sleepy blackness. I fought to focus, though, and soon realized I could see a light in the distance.

I drew closer to it. It was a window to the outside, and when I pressed my face to it, I could see my arms moving in complicated patterns and streams of icy blue energy pouring from my fingers. Bella shouted something, and the world tipped as my body jumped to the side to avoid another rush of fire. Flames shot by, close enough to singe, but I couldn't feel them, and I watched my left arm snap up, heard my voice roar out a command. A glowing barrier formed in front of me. My voice told Bella to stay behind me, and my body started to move forward.

The beckoning of the darkness was too tempting then, and I drifted into it and let myself rest. The distant light of the window faded and finally disappeared, and I slept.

*

I opened my eyes to Bella's worried face above me.

"Alisha?" she whispered. "Is it you?"

My mouth felt too dry, like I'd been chewing on cotton balls. I couldn't find my voice, so I just nodded. There was a sting of pain from my arm, and I glanced down to see a small burn on my left forearm, shiny and ugly in the morning light.

Bella helped me sit up with an arm around my shoulders. We were still in the field, and the possessed police officer stood literally frozen about ten feet away from us. Her body was encased in a twinkling layer of ice, and I could see from the murderous expression on her face and the way her hand was outstretched that she'd been getting ready to send a truly awful spell in our direction.

I shuddered. "I really did not enjoy that."

"Fun or not, it sure saved our asses." Bella's voice was unsteady, but her arms didn't shake as she helped me get to my feet. "Your dad's one hell of a spell caster. If your Grandma's even better than him, we might actually stand a chance of stopping these guys."

Dad? I thought worriedly. *You still there? You okay?*

I'm here was my dad's weary reply. *Completely wiped out, but I'll be okay. Are you all right?*

I think so. There was a lot to unpack in what had just happened to me, but that was going to have to wait until later. *Thanks. You saved us.*

Glad I could help, Dad said, and then I felt him retreating to the back of my mind again, probably to rest. I sure felt like I could use about a three-hour nap, but now definitely was not the time.

"I'm thinking we should leave before that spell wears off," I said, eyeing frozen Officer Shelby warily. "And probably before anybody else comes along and sees us."

"Agreed," Bella said.

We hurried across the tall grass, past Shelby, and out onto the road. The convertible sat there looking ludicrous as usual with its bright-red seats and sleek design, but I'd never been so happy to see it in my life. Shelby's cruiser was parked behind us with its four-ways flashing, and I wondered what the next person to pass by would think, coming upon a seemingly abandoned police car and what appeared to be a police officer ice sculpture in the field about twenty feet away. Hopefully, no one would notice until we'd gotten far, far away from here.

We buckled in, Bella revved the engine, and we sped off, the trunk flapping open and closed behind us.

"Okay," I said. My mind was racing right along with my adrenaline, and it was hard to keep my words from bubbling out in a rush. "That just happened, and I'm pretty sure it means the vesu know our plan, because it can't be a coincidence that we got pulled over like that on our way to the cave, can it?"

Bella chewed on her lower lip. "I don't know. Maybe they're just looking for us in general. If they've taken over some cops, they might just have them driving around looking for any sign of us. It doesn't necessarily mean they know what we're planning."

"They do," I said. "No way this was just a coincidence. They know what we're doing, and that means they know that my grandma, Uncle Lucas, my mom, and your mom are heading to headquarters right now to stop them. And if they know that—"

Bella's jaw clenched. Her hands tightened over the wheel as she spun us into a screeching U-turn that made my seat belt snap tight against my body.

"You better be sure about this," she said.

"I am."

The only thing I wasn't sure about was who had betrayed us.

Chapter Fifteen

Guardian headquarters was downtown in the shell of an old department store. A long time ago, people had flocked here at Christmastime for shopping, a parade, and a tree-lighting ceremony, but these days it was a faded white-brick building with pale-green trim around the windows and terracotta carving along the roof line. A liquor store stood guard at the base of the building, and other than that, the place looked like any other elderly building converted to office space, except there were no signs out front declaring what kinds of offices waited inside.

We parked a few streets down, since Bella's convertible was pretty conspicuous, and went the rest of the way on foot. It felt strange to be back here. Most of our training had been done at a separate training facility off in the middle of the woods, and I'd only ever been at HQ before for things like ceremonies and paperwork. The research team and the spell casting team were centered here, so Dad and Uncle Lucas spent a lot of their time in this building, but I'd never found it a particularly interesting place. Aside from the fact that the people inside it were fulfilling a sacred vow to protect the planet from any and all threats, it was still just a basic office building. People sat at desks, typed on computers, and drank coffee, and that kind of life was pretty far removed from why I'd decided to be a Guardian in the first place.

"So how do we do this?" Bella asked in an undertone. "Just barge in there, scream, 'It's a trap!' and peace out?"

A few other people were out on the sidewalk, and I couldn't help eyeing them warily, aware that any of them could be holding a vesu within them.

"Not exactly," I said quietly. "First priority is to find Uncle Lucas. He's the only one we can absolutely trust."

Bella's brow furrowed. "How do you—"

"Just trust me. I can't explain right now, but the vesu can't take him. My grandma was right about that. Anyway, once we find him, we'll tell him what happened and go from there."

Bella, instead of arguing, caught my hand and gave it a quick squeeze.

She didn't say anything, but she didn't need to. We both knew we were walking into an incredibly dangerous situation, into a place swarming with potential vesu and us with no way of telling who was one and who wasn't. Anyone could be an enemy, anyone could try to kill us, and that *anyone* might end up being someone we knew.

We strode through the front doors of the building and took the elevator up to the fourth floor. That was where the ceremonial chambers were and any big gathering of Guardians was bound to be held. Things seemed pretty normal as we stepped out onto the fourth floor's pale-blue carpeting. A young man sat at a reception desk talking to someone on the phone and tapping a pen against his desk, a few people in business casual power walked past holding clipboards, and somewhere in the distance I heard a phone ringing and someone shouting, "Hey, how old is this coffee?"

But there was tension in the air. I could feel it, and was it my imagination, or did more than a few gazes drift sideways to Bella and me as we passed, maybe not just with idle curiosity but with something more sinister? I was probably being paranoid, but since our new reality involved literal body snatchers, I figured I was entitled.

We made our way toward the largest of the ceremonial chambers since there was a definite steady flow of foot traffic in that direction, and we even saw a few other Guardians, also suited up in lightweight armor like we were, heading that way too. There was no sign of Uncle Lucas or Grandma or Mom, but I assumed they were already inside the chamber. For the first time, though, I started to wonder what we would do if we couldn't find them. What could Bella and I do against an unknown number of vesu whose attack might come at any moment, from any direction? Dad was an amazing spell caster, but even he couldn't take the whole vesu force on his own, and I wasn't anxious to let him take over my body again anyway.

We were a few hallways away from the chamber when there was a soft chime from the speaker system, and a soothing voice said, "Emergency meeting will be starting in five minutes. Please make your way to Chamber One on the fourth floor for briefing."

Bella and I exchanged nervous glances. Five minutes wasn't long to find Uncle Lucas, tell him what had happened, and figure out what to do. By mutual unspoken agreement, we quickened our pace and soon joined a line of people shuffling forward to enter the chamber. To my surprise, the chamber entrance was flanked by two Guardians and a spell caster, the Guardians standing on either side with their arms crossed while the spell caster spoke a few words with each person before allowing them to enter.

"What is that about, do you think?" Bella murmured.

I shook my head, figuring we would find out soon enough. The line moved speedily, and before long it was my turn. I stepped up to the doorway and met the gaze of the spell caster, a young woman with long dreadlocks and a solemn expression. She waved a hand in front of my face and murmured a few words, then met my eyes.

"Are you a human being and a true member of the Guardians?" she asked.

I frowned, but of course I said, "Yes."

There was a sparkle of blue light from the air in front of my face, and I realized she'd cast some sort of truth spell. Which was a good idea but would have been better if truth spells weren't notoriously unreliable. But hey, better than nothing?

The spell caster nodded me into the chamber, so I moved past her and lingered in the doorway until Bella likewise received the all clear, and we stepped into the chamber together.

It was pretty impressive, I had to admit. Long rows of velvet cushioned benches formed a semicircle that led up to the stage, a huge platform of polished wood with a podium, some tasteful potted plants, and a banner with the Guardians symbol—the planet Earth being held by a protective pair of hands—pinned to the wall behind it. Many of the bench seats were already filled with Guardians, spell casters, researchers, data team members, and assistants, and I could make out a few council members seated front row center, waiting for the proceedings to begin. I caught sight of Lettie's bubblegum-pink hair over on the left-hand side of the room and wondered if she was still herself, or if she was among the people who'd been taken.

How many of these people were vesu? There was no way to know, and I felt a chill that had nothing to do with the overly aggressive air-conditioning system. I couldn't see Uncle Lucas, Mom, or Grandma anywhere, and from the way she was frowning, Bella couldn't either. We had to keep up with the flow of traffic, though, so we made our way down the aisle, and every second I was sure their faces were going to jump out at me, but they never did. Finally, we got so close to the stage that we had to stop and turn around.

"They're not here," I whispered.

"Where else could they be?"

"Maybe they got pulled over like we did and got—" I broke off, not wanting to finish the sentence. *Captured? Killed? Worse?*

"Or maybe they're here but not here-in-this-room. Maybe they're doing it from somewhere else, somewhere hidden. I mean, they can't very well cast a big freaking spell right here in this chamber, can they?"

"Should we go back out? Try to find them?"

"Let's sit in the back, by the door." Bella took my arm and pulled me back up the aisle even though we were going against the flow of bodies. "They still might be coming. And at least we can run for it if things go south."

This wasn't the best plan, but I couldn't think of anything better, so I followed Bella to a handy pair of seats right next to the door we'd come in through. I wondered what would happen if anyone failed the spell caster's truth test, but the thought only hung in my mind for a second before it was pushed out by another chorus of, *Where are they?*

I dug my phone out of my pocket. I'd sent both Uncle Lucas and Mom a text message in the car, and so far neither of them had replied. I hesitated, then brought up my texts to Uncle Lucas and typed another message.

We're in the chamber. No sign of you guys. Where are you??
Send.

Text me back, I thought desperately toward Uncle Lucas. *Text me so I know you're okay. Please…*

The lights flickered off and on, off and on, and the chatter of the room died down to a murmur. There was an expectant hush as we all gazed up at the stage, and then a tall, red-robed figure approached the podium. It was Gideon Jones, one of the elder members of the council, and I knew by the gold sash adorning his robes that he'd taken on the role of head of the council in Martina's absence.

"Gideon," Bella muttered. "Just what we need."

I hadn't had any real encounters with Gideon, but it was easy to see he was nowhere near as tough and put together as Martina. Gideon was blond and a bit doughy and had an air of hesitancy about him. As he stood at the podium, he didn't seem to know where to put his hands, first dropping them to his sides, then sliding them into the pockets of his robes, then gripping the edges of the podium as if for support.

"Thank you all for coming." He had a low, froggy sort of voice, the kind that made me want to clear my throat. "You're all aware of the situation by now. Through the negligence of my predecessor, Martina Rodriguez, our world is now under attack."

Bella bristled beside me. I gripped her hand in hopes that she wouldn't do or say anything to get us noticed.

"In an operation entirely unsanctioned by the Guardians organization, Ms. Rodriguez and a traitor spell caster opened up a rift between our world and one of the dark dimensions, and now the vesu have succeeded in breaking into our world."

I stared at him in shock. A traitor? Did he mean my dad?

"This situation is especially dire since we're dealing with incorporeal entities that can take over a host and eject that host's spirit from its body in the process. We're uncertain at this time just how many of the creatures have entered our world, but it's certainly a sufficient number for them to have infiltrated our organization. There's a good chance that a body possessed by a vesu sits in this very room. Probably more than one."

A murmur went through the chamber, and people exchanged wary glances. Bella's fingers tightened over mine, and I clung to hers just as tightly.

"Fortunately, this kind of situation is not without precedent, if not in our world, then certainly in others. In consulting the intelligence we've gathered from other dimensions, our spell casters have happened upon a method of purging the vesu from our world, and we'll start by purging them from this room."

I exchanged frowns with Bella, wondering what Gideon had in mind, but she looked as confused as I did.

Gideon gestured, and a line of blue-robed spell casters rose from their seats and filed up to the stage. They each held a sealed wooden box, the same kind I'd seen sitting on the dresser in Grandma's big bedroom only a few hours earlier. In that case, the box had contained a captured vesu.

"These boxes," Gideon continued, "contain spirits that can locate the vesu. The spell casters have summoned them here for this specific purpose, at my command. When released, the spirits will home in on those with vesu inside them and force the vesu out, essentially using the creatures' own tactics against them."

"Is this for real?" Bella whispered.

"I doubt it," I whispered back. "I'm pretty sure there are vesu in those boxes, and they're about to take over everyone in this room."

"Including us. We have to get out of here."

I opened my mouth to suggest we warn everyone first, then immediately thought better of it. What would happen if we stood and shouted that the vesu were here and were going to try to take over everyone in this room? The spell casters would just open the boxes and send vesu pouring out, and everyone would get taken anyway.

And Bella and I would lose our chance to escape.

Both of us looked to the nearby door as nonchalantly as we could. Two Guardians had taken up positions with their backs to the doors, and they weren't teens but women in their thirties or forties who seemed made out of muscle.

"You up for a fight?" I said.

Bella gave a flicker of her old smirk. "Always."

On the stage, the spell casters stepped forward with their boxes. Gideon stood to one side, looking pompously pleased with himself and his leadership, and there was a general murmur from the audience. Some of the murmurs were confused, questioning, but no one seemed to want to speak up too loudly for fear of being thought a vesu.

A tall red-haired spell caster took a step forward. "Brothers, sisters, we release you," she intoned, which was not a creepy thing to say at all. "We free you from your torment and give you the promise of a new life!"

"Oh, God," Bella breathed.

The spell casters chanted a few words, undoing the binding spells keeping the boxes sealed, and flung open the lids.

Shadowy forms poured from the boxes, screeching and cackling and not sounding at all like spirits who had come to help us. One of them immediately surged into Gideon, who shrieked and began contorting and twitching as the spirit took over his body. People all over the room leapt to their feet, some pulling out weapons, some beginning to chant spells, but the vesu were already streaming forward and slamming into body after body, taking over the Guardians one by one.

Even though I'd known what was coming, it was still hard not to stay frozen there staring in horror. Instead, I launched myself from my seat and at the nearest Guardian by the door. She'd been standing with her arms folded, a smirk on her face as she enjoyed the show, and it was clear she hadn't expected someone to come flying out of nowhere, get an arm around her neck, and hurl her to the ground.

But I did it, and man, did it feel good.

Her head hit the floor hard enough to knock her out, which suited me just fine. I leapt to my feet and turned to face the other Guardian, but Bella was already on it. She swept the woman's leg and knocked her flat onto her back, giving her a swift punch to the jaw to further seal the deal. Before the woman could recover, Bella and I were out the door and sprinting down the deserted hallway.

Screams echoed behind us, and my heart hammered in my ears as I realized that while we'd technically escaped from the chamber, there were still vesu free and looking for bodies, and they could track us down at any second. Not to mention that we seemed to be on course for the entire local body of the Guardians to be taken over, and that was pretty much the worst thing that could possibly have happened.

Dad, I thought, wondering if maybe he could do some kind of barrier spell to protect us while we looked for Uncle Lucas, Mom, and Grandma. *Dad, are you there?*

But there was no answer, Dad presumably still out of commission from his earlier spellcasting, so I clenched my jaw and kept running.

"Where are we going?" Bella gasped as we turned down another identical hallway.

"I don't know," I gasped back. "Stairwell?"

It probably wasn't a great idea to stay on this floor, and while going up or down was unlikely to hide us from flying shadow monsters, at least it might keep them from finding us for a while.

We made it to the stairwell and decided to go up. Anyone pursuing us on foot would most likely assume we'd gone down, since getting out of the building made sense in terms of escaping, but I knew we couldn't leave until we'd figured out what had happened to Grandma, Uncle Lucas, and Mom. Where were they? Had they already been taken? If they had, where was Uncle Lucas?

We ended up on the eighth floor, which had been undergoing renovations since time immemorial. Tarps were spread out over the carpet, a ladder led up to a removed ceiling tile, and a dusty toolbox sat by the window. No workers were in sight, and the lights were off. The only illumination came through the closed blinds on the windows, giving the place a dim, abandoned look. There was no furniture but a lot of empty rooms, so it seemed a good place to hide out for the time being.

As we looked around, I pulled out my phone and tapped out one more message to Uncle Lucas.

The vesu are here. Pretty sure all the other Guardians have been taken. Where are you?

I hit Send. I'd only taken a few steps, though, when my pocket vibrated. I almost dropped my phone in my hurry to pull it out.

We know, was the reply. *Are you all right? Where are you?*

"Did he text back?" Bella said.

I nodded, but I couldn't help frowning. Answering "Where are you?" with the question "Where are you?" wasn't exactly what I'd been hoping he would do.

We're safe for now, I sent.

A pause of maybe three seconds, then another buzz:

Where are you??

I slid the phone back into my pocket, feeling cold inside.

"I think someone got his phone." The words felt like ashes on my tongue because if someone had gotten his phone, someone had gotten him.

I could see my own fear reflected in Bella's face, and I knew she knew what this meant. If they'd taken Uncle Lucas, then they'd probably taken Mom and Martina and Grandma too.

We were alone.

Chapter Sixteen

We wandered through the abandoned eighth floor like lost souls, glancing into empty offices but never stopping, just walking and walking. Maybe because stopping somewhere would mean we had to figure out what to do next, and I for one had no freaking idea.

I would've been okay with walking forever, but our steps eventually led us to a hallway that dead-ended, and we came to a stop facing the wall.

Dead end. Appropriate.

I was about to suggest we turn around, maybe try to get out of the building and back to Jake, Aggie, and Gwen, when I heard something. I frowned, drawing closer to the wall. I could hear soft, distant voices through it, which should've been impossible since this was, as previously mentioned, a pretty clear and obvious dead end.

Not daring to speak, I nodded my head in the direction of the wall and mimed listening. Bella tilted her head toward the wall—then snapped back from it, her eyes widening.

Someone was here, on the abandoned eighth floor.

I pressed my hands against the wall, not sure what I was looking for but sure I was looking for something, and eventually I found it. A decorative strip of wood bisected the wall between floor and ceiling, and when I touched it, it slid up to reveal a black panel underneath.

It was a keypad.

I looked at Bella questioningly, and she stepped forward with unexpected confidence and typed a few numbers into the pad. I waited for an alarm to go off or for someone to come running, but instead the panel gave a pleased chime and a door opened in the wall to reveal a dark hallway beyond.

I wanted to say, "What kind of Nancy Drew crap is this?" but I knew we didn't dare risk being overheard, so instead I shook my head and stepped into the hallway with Bella, promising myself I'd ask her about the code later. If there was a later, of course.

Unlike the rest of the floor, which had standard, boring office carpeting, this section had a smooth white floor, probably not marble but at least marble-like. Everything was white from floor to ceiling, giving the place a cold, sterile feeling, and there was light from somewhere up ahead. Light probably meant people, but what else could we do?

We walked toward the light.

To our credit, we walked sneakily and quietly toward the light, and when we came to a doorway that seemed to lead into a larger room, we took cover on either side of it and peered inside like good, stealthy Guardians.

It was a large, round room, all white like the hallway and with some sci-fi-ish computer panels and a few metal carts with weird metal instruments on them. I barely noticed them, though, because what stood in the center of the room wouldn't let me look anywhere else.

It was a large tube of shimmering blue light that extended from the floor all the way to the ceiling. It looked like some kind of containment spell, and inside it was a girl.

She looked around my age, maybe a year or two younger, and she had long dark hair and wore a hooded gray sweatshirt, blue jeans, and sneakers. She was hovering in midair, arms out, head tilted back, and eyes closed, floating there peacefully as if suspended in liquid.

I hadn't gotten over my shock yet when I realized Bella had left the shadows and was moving out into the room.

"Bella!" I whispered after her, but she swept forward like someone caught in a dream, her eyes locked on the floating girl inside the barrier.

"Marigold?" she said incredulously.

I looked from Bella to the girl and back again, then dared to draw out of the shadows. "You know her?"

I was surprised to see a mist of tears in Bella's eyes. "Yeah. That's my sister."

Marigold. Mari. I studied the girl more closely and saw the resemblance to the portrait in the Rodriguez's abandoned sitting room, and the resemblance to Bella herself.

I must've still been in some kind of shock, because the only thing I could think of to say at this bizarre revelation was, "Her name is Marigold?"

Bella threw me an irritated glance. "They named me 'Daisy.' What do you expect?"

"So, what's she doing here? And what is all this?"

"I don't know. I thought that maybe the cave had something to do with her disappearing, but now here she is, floating in some secret room in Guardian headquarters? It doesn't make sense. And look at her! It's been five years, but she looks exactly the same. It's like she hasn't aged. What did my mom do to her?"

"How do you know your mom did this?"

Bella glanced back the way we'd come. "That keypad. My mom had the same one installed on her office door at home."

"She has a keypad lock on her office door?"

A flicker of annoyance touched Bella's expression. "She never tells me anything, so I have to find things out on my own. I guess she finally figured out I was going through her files and hacking into her council meetings, because she installed the keypad and some new firewall software on her computer. The firewall was a joke, and it only took me a day or two to crack the keypad. She used the same code here." Her voice grew softer and a bit distant. "She uses the same password for everything too. You'd think the head of the council would be smarter than that."

I shook my head and found myself at an utter loss for words. My family was missing, the vesu had just taken over Guardians HQ, and now we'd found Bella's older sister, who had been missing for five years and apparently hadn't aged a day in all that time, inexplicably suspended inside a magical force field in a secret room on the eighth floor. Sure. Why not? Why not.

Bella drew forward and held her hand up to the barrier. "We have to get her out of here. I don't know what this is or why Mom did this, but she's my sister and I can't leave her here." She looked back at me with pleading eyes, as if begging me to understand, but I already did.

"Let's do it," I said. "Do you know how to dismantle all this?"

"I think so. This can't be a normal spell, or it'd never be able to stay in place for so long without a spell caster present, so it must be supported by these computers. Spells, I don't know much about, but computers? I can figure this out."

She leaned over one of the consoles and started tapping away at an impressive speed, and a few minutes passed with no sound but the patter of her fingers on the panel.

"There. I think I got it."

We both turned to look at the barrier around Mari, and sure enough, something was happening to it. The shimmering blue began to tremble, a ripple went through it like a wave, and then the barrier vanished, and Mari dropped limply to the floor.

Bella was at her side in an instant, drawing her sister into a sitting position against her and saying her name, touching her face. I stood back at a respectful distance, not wanting to intrude, and wondered uneasily where the people whose voices we'd heard earlier had gone. I was about to suggest we support Mari between us and hightail it out of there when Dad's voice echoed in my head.

Oh, Alisha, what have you done?

He did not sound happy. He sounded, in fact, the opposite of happy.

What do you mean? They were holding Bella's sister here, so we got her out, and—

Sweetheart, that's not Bella's sister. Not anymore.

Mari had been coming around, and before I could process my dad's words, her eyes fluttered open, and she stared up at Belladonna's face.

"Bella?" she murmured.

Bella smiled and wiped her eyes. "Hey. Yeah. It's me. Long time no see, huh?"

Mari smiled too, but there was something almost predatory about it. Bella was busy helping her sister to her feet and didn't seem to notice, and while I still didn't know exactly what was going on, it was becoming clear that there was a damn good reason why Martina had been keeping Mari floating unconscious in a secret room. I took a step forward to say something—

And froze. Not because I'd told my limbs to freeze, but because Mari had waved a casual hand in my direction, and just like that, my body had stopped moving. I couldn't speak, and I couldn't move a muscle.

Dad, what's going on? I asked desperately.

Mari didn't disappear, Alisha. She was taken over by the vesu. They'd been communicating with her through the dimensional weak spot in the cave, and they convinced her that they were friendly, that they needed her help. Her magic was powerful enough to open a rift in the cave wall, but she wasn't strong enough to hold it open for more than a second. That one second was enough for one of the vesu to come through and take her. Her spirit was sucked back into the rift as it closed.

We've been trying to get her spirit back for years, but we just couldn't find a way to do it without bringing more of the vesu along with her. Your Uncle Lucas brought back some spells from Argentina that seemed like they could help us, but— Well, you know what happened when we tried them.

I stared at Bella and Mari in horror. *How is she doing this to me?*

The vesu that took Mari isn't like the others, Dad said. *It's strong, particularly in magic. If we hadn't captured it, it probably would've opened a thousand gateways to the dark dimensions by now. And now that it's free...*

I fought against the invisible bonds that held me, but it was no use. All I could do was blink and breathe, and stare at Bella as if willing her to turn around and see me, to see what Mari had done to me. But Mari had her full attention.

"I really have to thank you," Mari said, reaching up to caress Bella's face with her slender fingers. "The others had been trying to get me out of there for hours, but they couldn't seem to manage it. How lucky for us that you came along."

Bella frowned. "What do you mean? What others?"

A door opened at the far end of the room and two figures walked in—Martina and my dad, or at least the vesu-controlled versions of them. It still looked like my dad, with the sandy hair, bushy eyebrows, mustache, and polo shirt, but the way he was walking was all wrong, and the look on his face and in his eyes... It wasn't him. I'd never realized before how much of my dad's personality shone out from his face, but now it was obvious that it did, and this was not him.

Martina gave us a thin-lipped smile. "Well, it looks as if you've done what we couldn't do and released our lost sister."

Bella stared at her in confusion, and for the first time, she glanced at me and seemed to realize something was off. "Howard?" Her head snapped back to Martina. "What do you mean, *your* sister?"

Mari gave Bella a quick, sisterly side hug before taking a step away from her. "I've been in stasis for years, so the memory of how to release me wasn't in anyone's short-term memory. No way for my brothers and sisters to access it in the minds they took over. If you hadn't come along, it might have taken days to figure out how to free me, or longer. Thank you, sister. This will all go so much more smoothly now because of your help. And thank you to you too," she said, nodding graciously at me. She gestured and I sank to my hands and knees, gasping for breath and sweating. "I wasn't sure my magic was still up to par after all these years, but it seems to be as strong as ever."

"Bella, she's a vesu!" I said when I could speak. "They got her in the cave all those years ago!"

The color drained from Bella's face. "What? No. That—that can't be. Then where—?" She turned to Mari with rage and pain in her eyes. "Where's my sister?"

"Oh, long gone," Mari said. "Her spirit was drawn into my dimension as the rift closed, so I imagine she's still there. Pity. I doubt she's enjoying it." She turned from Bella as if she'd lost interest in her and faced Martina and my dad. "Are the preparations complete?"

To my surprise, the two vesu bowed their heads to her as if in respect.

"They are," Martina said. "All below have been taken. They await your command."

Mari smiled. "Good. Once I've opened the rift, they'll have lots of company."

Dad? I think we might be in big trouble here.

Honey, Dad replied. *I think you're right.*

*

They tied us up, which I couldn't help thinking was kind of a silly thing to do when there were things like magical cages and body-stealing creatures from another dimension floating around. Mari explained to us, in a kind and conversational tone, that while all the bodiless vesu in the vicinity had found other hosts, there would shortly be an abundance in search of bodies, at which point we would no longer be neglected.

"You don't have to do this," I said as our hands and feet were bound, because someone had to say it. "Things are awful in your dimension. I get it. I'm sure we can find you guys a nicer place to live that doesn't involve quite so much, you know, torment."

To my surprise, Mari's eyes flashed with anger. "What do you know about it? You live in this paradise world, possessing your own body and your own free will, able to live and die as you choose. We have no such choice. Every day of our existence is agony. Every moment is torture. We exist in endless darkness, wandering and lost with no release of death to save us. Many have lost their minds, but some of us fight to find a way out. We made contact with other beings and discovered that gateways could be opened to other worlds. Imagine our surprise when we learned that worlds like this existed, and that the beings fortunate enough to exist here don't even realize how unjustly fortunate they are. What makes your people more deserving of life and peace than mine? What makes your lives more worthy than ours?"

"Nothing," I said. "But we're not trying to destroy your people. You're trying to destroy us."

"Honestly?" Mari leaned so close to me that I thought I could see the shadows of the vesu swirling deep in the pupils of her eyes. "If destroying your people means saving mine, then I welcome your destruction."

The three of them left shortly thereafter, and Bella and I found ourselves sitting bound and gagged in the sterile chamber that had been Mari's prison. I waited a few minutes after the door had closed behind them, then took a deep breath that smelled like the musty fabric of my gag.

There was an obvious solution to this, an obvious way to escape, but it scared the crap out of me. Still, if the alternative was hanging out here tied up while Mari opened up the rift and vesu took over the world, what was a little discomfort and existential terror, right?

Dad, I need you to take control of me again and cast a spell to get us out of this.

There was a long silence.

Dad!

I'm here, sweetie. I'm just— I'm thinking.

About?

About how much energy it took to cast spells through you the last time, and how long it took me to recover. I'm still not recovered, if you want to know the truth. If I do this, I might be out of commission for a long time, and if you need help later on, I won't be able to do anything.

Dad, there won't be a later if we don't get out of here right now!

There was another silence.

All right. Give me control.

Sinking down into myself was just as unsettling as it had been the first time, but I knew it had to be done. I drifted in the darkness, out of control of my body for the second time that day, and prayed Dad would be strong enough to get us out of this.

Much more quickly than last time, I felt myself rising, floating—

I opened my eyes and fought an overwhelming rush of vertigo. My hand slapped out against the wall to steady me, which probably meant I was no longer tied up.

I held my hands out in front of my face, and they were, indeed, free. The thick plastic tie that had held my wrists lay singed and smoking on the floor by my feet, and while my ankles were still bound, that didn't present too much of a problem. I figured Dad hadn't wanted to risk doing any more than the bare minimum of spell casting, and as I pulled a pocketknife out of, of course, my pocket, I sent a querying, *Dad?* into the dark depths of my mind.

There was no answer. I hoped he was just resting, but there was nothing I could do either way, so I focused on cutting the bonds from my ankles, then hurried over to Bella's side to free her too.

She was crying, tears streaming down her face, and her breath coming harshly through the cloth of the gag. I'd never seen her so out of control before, and the sight of her wet cheeks and anguished eyes froze me as effectively as Mari's spell had done. My chest ached with the sudden wish that I could take the pain away from her, but I knew that was one thing I couldn't do. What I could do was use my knife to cut away her bonds, then carefully pull the gag away from her mouth.

She sniffled a few times and wiped a hand over her face.

"They took my mom," she said in a trembling voice. The emotion I was hearing in her words wasn't despair. It was rage. "And now I find out that they took my sister too." Her dark eyes snapped up to mine, fury boiling within them. "We have to take them down. We have to take them *out*."

"That's exactly what we're going to do," I said.

We made it through the secret door and back to the stairwell unmolested, and from the utter stillness around us, I gathered Mari and company had already left.

We raced down the stairs as quickly as we could go without risking a fall—a broken bone was the last thing we needed right now—and burst out into the daylight after eight long flights. The stairwell door let us out in the alley, which suited us just fine. The air was fresh and crisp, like the seasons had debated the issue and decided on fall after all, and the sun was still shining as we ducked out of the alley and raced down the sidewalk toward Bella's convertible.

No one else was around, which was definitely not normal for this time of day in the center of downtown. I wondered where everyone was, if the vesu takeover had extended beyond Guardians HQ and had taken everyone in the vicinity too. It was impossible to know how many vesu had come through the rift since last night, or how many innocent people they had taken over.

Bella had us in drive and speeding down the road the second the car doors closed, and I fumbled for my seat belt while we bumped and jolted over a series of potholes.

"Head for my grandma's house," I said.

"Your grandma's house? You think we have time for a piece of pie or something? The *world* is going to end. We have to get to the cave."

"My grandma has spell books, ancient ones. They'll tell us how to close that rift."

"What about your dad?" Bella asked. "I thought he knew how to do that too."

"He does, but I can't reach him."

"What do you mean? Where is he?"

"He's still there, but taking control of my body takes a lot of energy, and it takes him a long time to recover. We might not be able to depend on him when we get to the cave."

"Then who the hell is going to close that rift?"

I gave a tight smile. "Aggie."

Chapter Seventeen

Aggie had always taken after Dad. She had his sense of humor, his kindness, and his ability to see the good in all the people of the world. She also, as it happened, had inherited some of his magic.

Dad had tried teaching spell casting to all three of us kids, but Aggie was the only one who'd taken to it. I was more interested in the physical side of things, and Jake just wanted to read his comics and go exploring outside—he didn't have the patience to sit around chanting weird words trying to get a pencil to roll across the table.

But Aggie? Aggie was a natural.

She'd picked it up so quickly that I'd once overheard my mom telling my dad that she was a little scared by it, afraid Aggie would end up with more power than she had the judgment or maturity to deal with responsibly. She was only twelve at the time, but when Dad took her to Guardians HQ to meet the head of the spell casters, Aggie blew her away—literally. Wind spell, *whoosh*.

It had been pretty clear that Aggie was going to follow in Dad's footsteps and join the Guardians' spell casting squad, but that wasn't what happened.

There'd been some bullies at the park picking on a bunch of younger kids. Shoving them, pushing them down, laughing at them, making them cry. Aggie had stood up to the bullies, and they'd turned on her. She was a skinny little girl with glasses, and they were older and bigger and not afraid to use their fists, and there were four of them. The magic poured out of her in self-defense, and one kid was left with third-degree burns while another ended up with a broken arm and partial hearing loss in one ear. Permanent damage. The Guardians PR team had spun a pretty good story to the press and the parents about a freak lightning strike causing the whole thing, but the damage had still been done. And it had been done by Aggie, the kindest human being in the world.

Aggie was horrified. Magic had done this, and so she didn't want to do magic anymore. She gave it up, and no matter how many times Dad tried to talk her out of her decision, even years later, she stuck by it. Magic hurt people, and she didn't want to hurt people, so she wasn't going to use it anymore.

She'd made a vow, just like Grandma had. I could only pray that, like Grandma, she wouldn't mind breaking it.

*

We pulled into Grandma's driveway with a crunch of gravel and surveyed the house. It looked completely normal and still, but that didn't mean a thing. I could only pray the barrier was still up. If it was, then Jake, Aggie, and Gwen were safe in there. If it wasn't...

No, I told myself firmly. *Enough has gone wrong today. This is one damn thing that is going to go right.*

We leapt out of the car and ran toward the porch. Grandma had said the barrier would have enough juice to stay in place for at least four or five hours, so it should still be up. As we moved, I grabbed a stone from the driveway and threw it at the house.

It struck something midair and shimmered, and I heaved a sigh of relief. They were safe.

"Aggie!" I shouted. "Jake! Gwen!"

It was a weird redo and reversal of Gwen's arrival earlier, Jake, Aggie, and Gwen pouring out onto the porch while Bella and I stood beyond the barrier looking in.

Aggie took charge, coming to the porch railing and looking out at us carefully. "What are you guys doing back here?"

The words poured out of me. "Everything went wrong. Bella and I got pulled over on the way to the cave, and the cop turned out to be a vesu and tried to kill us, but we got away and went to headquarters, and the vesu took over everyone there, *everyone*. I can't get in touch with Uncle Lucas or Mom or Grandma, and I'm pretty sure they got taken too. And we found Bella's sister, and it turns out she's been a vesu for years and she's going to the cave to open up the rift because she's really good at magic, and so we're here to get you to come with us to the cave and help us seal it up before the whole world gets taken over. And if you're wondering why we need you to do that, it's because Dad's tired out because he took over my body so we could escape, and now I don't think he'll be able to help us so it's all on us, and on you. I know that's not what you want, and you swore never to use magic again, but there's literally no one else who can do it, so I really hope you will."

There was a long silence, and I could feel Bella staring at me.

"How did you do that without taking a breath?" she said.

"I was breathing," I shot back.

"How do we know it's really you?" Jake shouted from behind Aggie. He was holding hands with Gwen, who was studying me cautiously.

Aggie sighed and waved her hand, and a doorway opened in the barrier to let us through.

"It's Alisha," she said. "No way a vesu could babble like that."

"Thanks," I said, and we hugged. She should've asked me some questions to make absolutely sure it was me, but there was no time to spare, so I didn't bring it up. "We have to get Grandma's books and then get to the cave as fast as we can."

"Okay," Aggie said. "I didn't understand most of what you said just now, but you can fill me in on the way."

"You can fill *us* in on the way," Jake said, and Aggie and I both turned to him with older sister firmness.

"No," I said.

"Jake, you and Gwen are not coming," Aggie said.

"The heck we're not! Look, if things are as bad as you guys say, then you're gonna need all the help you can get. We might not be able to do magic and junk, but we can fight or stand guard or *something*. If Mom and Grandma and Uncle Lucas are out of commission, then we're all we've got. Right?"

And he was right. I shifted my gaze to Gwen. "Are you sure you want to come too? No shame at all in staying here."

Gwen fixed me with a steady stare. "I'm coming. After what they did to me, I'd kind of like the chance to dish out some payback."

I sighed. "All right. Fine. I guess we're all going, then. Get anything that could be used as a weapon and put it in the car."

Bella and I trooped upstairs after Aggie, and we found her on her way down the attic stairs with an armful of dusty tomes.

"Dad let me look at these once or twice," she said, "but I was never allowed to read them on my own. There's some pretty powerful stuff in here. I'll go through them on the way, but I think I already know what kind of spell we'll need."

We headed downstairs and found Gwen in the kitchen throwing bottles of water into a cloth shopping bag.

"Saving the world is thirsty work," she said, which reminded me of how ridiculously dry my throat was. I held out my hand, and she slapped a water bottle into it. I poured cool, clean liquid down my throat until the bottle was nearly empty.

Gwen smiled at me. "Better?"

"So much." And because everything was crazy and we had no idea what was going to happen, I pulled her into a hug and held her close. She hugged me back, hard, and then we released each other and went out to the car.

Bella and I sat in front while Aggie, Jake, and Gwen squeezed into the back seat, Aggie with her glasses pushed far up on her nose as she stared down at the pages of one of the spell books. Jake had his arm around Gwen, Gwen leaning her head lightly against his, and I prayed we hadn't made a huge mistake in letting them come with us.

We backed out of the driveway and sped off for the cave.

Chapter Eighteen

"Well," I said, putting down the binoculars Gwen had been smart enough to grab on the way out of the house. "This makes things a little bit tougher."

I hadn't been sure what to expect, but it definitely hadn't been this. We'd come most of the way down the trail without seeing anyone, but as we'd gotten closer to the mouth of the cave, it had become pretty clear that something was going on up ahead. And, boy, something was.

We'd ducked into the cover of a copse of trees on the hillside and hidden there. Bella, Jake, Aggie, Gwen, and I crouched in the foliage, peering at the trail up ahead. People in police uniforms milled around the trail outside the cave, and they'd even gone so far as to put up caution tape to make the whole thing seem more legit. Three tough-looking Guardians stood on the ledge outside the mouth of the cave, and I recognized Claire Grayson's square jaw and cropped white-blonde hair.

"So, what do we do?" Jake said. His crouch had a bit too much bounce to it, as if any second he might launch himself at the crowd of vesu-controlled cops and Guardians. "Rush 'em? Cast a spell and sweep them all into the river?"

I put my hand on his shoulder. "No. That is not what we're going to do."

"And I'm not sweeping anyone into the river," Aggie said. "I'm only using magic when it's absolutely necessary. We'll just have to figure something else out."

"If only there was another way in or something," I said.

Jake's face went suddenly blank.

"What?"

"Oh, my God," he said.

I looked around, sure we were about to be attacked. "*What?*"

"Oh, my God, I'm so dumb!"

"You're just now realizing that?" Gwen said in a fond voice.

"No, I mean— I've been here before. To this cave. And there is an-other entrance."

We all stared at him.

"Are you sure?" I asked. "Are you absolutely, absolutely sure?"

"I'm sure!" he said. "It's around the back. You can only get to it if you go through the woods, and it's all overgrown and stuff. You can't see it unless you know where it is."

"And are you sure it's *this* cave, this same exact one?"

"I mean, I'm not one hundred percent sure, and it was a long time ago, but I'm ninety-seven percent sure it's the same one. Ninety-eight? Ninety-eight percent. Definitely."

I studied his face closely. It was true that Jake was a big fan of exploring the woods around here, and the centipede monster's lair cer-tainly wasn't the first cave he'd ventured into. I remembered a much younger Jake vanishing for hours and coming back with leaves in his hair, dirt on the knees of his pants, and a secretive grin on his face. We'd been best friends growing up, but he'd still never told me all the secret places he'd found in his explorations. Maybe this was one of them.

What I didn't want to think about was that Bella's sister had probably found the cave around that same general time. What if the vesu had been calling to anyone in the area sensitive enough to pick up on their message? What if Jake had picked up on that call, and that's why both he and Mari had found their way to it? I felt suddenly cold at the realization that it could've been Jake, not Mari, suspended in a magical stasis field for all these years. I mean, granted, Jake wouldn't have had anywhere near the magical ability necessary to open a rift in the dimensional wall, but the idea of the vesu calling to my—at the time—innocent little brother gave me a serious case of the shivers.

I turned to Bella. "What do you think?"

She'd been sitting silently by, watching us and chewing on her lip.

"I think we don't have a lot of options, and if there really is another way in, it'd make this whole thing a lot easier."

I nodded. "All right, Jake. Take us to this other entrance."

We crept away, but I could hear Jake chuckling softly to himself, and when we'd moved far enough down the trail not to fear the vesu hearing us, he nudged me with his shoulder. "See, aren't you glad I came along?"

I rolled my eyes and nudged him back. "Find this secret entrance first, and then I'll be glad."

Jake pretended to look wounded, but I could tell he was fighting a smile. He was actually able to do something to help for once, and I knew how much that must mean to him. The poor guy was the only semi-normal person in the whole family, the only one who couldn't fight or cast spells, and that had to wear at him. Maybe that was why he'd spent so much time exploring on his own when he was a kid. Maybe he'd been trying to find what made him special.

Maybe I was just getting sentimental. Whatever the case, I was glad we'd brought him along, not just because he knew about the cave's other entrance, but because there was something endlessly buoyant about Jake that always made me feel a little better than I had before. He was an optimist, something I'd never been particularly good at, and after everything that had happened, optimism was a pretty good thing to have.

Once we got back to the car, Jake told Bella where to drive and we parked a few streets down near the edge of the woods. We were on the other side of the hill that bordered the riverside trail, and as Jake led us through the trees, I thought with a tingle of excitement that we did seem to be going in the same direction as the cave.

It took us about fifteen minutes to get there, and there was a long period when I was sure Jake had no idea where he was going and we were going to still be wandering there at nightfall when all the vesu came pouring out to get us. This didn't last too long, though, and soon the look of confidence returned to his face and he led us straight to a dense thicket of overgrowth on the hillside.

"This is it," he said.

We eyed it doubtfully. It just looked like a clump of tangled bushes and weeds, but when Jake pushed some of them aside, we found ourselves looking at what was, unmistakably, the mouth to a cave.

It was smaller than the other entrance—we'd have to crawl through it for sure—but it was a circular opening lined in gray stone, and I could feel the coolness seeping from inside. This was it. This was our way in.

I wrapped my arm around Jake's neck and pulled him in for a hug-slash-headlock. Before releasing him, I kissed the top of his curly head and said, "*Now* I'm glad you came."

As I looked at the cave mouth, though, my jubilant feelings melted away.

"All right," I said quietly. "We don't know where this is going to lead us, or how easy it'll be to find the chamber with the rift in it. There might be vesu anywhere, with bodies or without. I'm not gonna lie, this is probably the most dangerous thing we've ever done, and we might—We might not—"

Bella clapped her hand on my shoulder and squeezed it. "Hell of a pep talk, Howard. Look, here's the deal. These bastards are taking people we love, and they're not going to stop unless we stop them. Are we ready to take them down?"

There was a general—though carefully quiet—cry of "Yeah!" and I had to admit that this was a slightly better way of rousing the troops than my own speech had been.

"Okay, let's go," I said. "Single file; then we'll spread out when the cave opens up. Stay together and stay quiet."

I went first, crawling into the cave on my belly with Bella's mini-flashlight held tight in my hand. Next came Aggie, Jake, and Gwen, and Bella brought up the rear since we'd agreed it made sense to have someone at each end who was capable of fighting. The cave floor was, as expected, cold and hard and a little damp, but after a few minutes of crawling on our bellies, we were able to rise to hands and knees, then walk in a crouch, and then finally stand.

No one else seemed to be around, and I wondered if we really had found the right cave, and if we had, how long it would be before we found the chamber, or if someone would find us first.

We crept along in eerie silence. All I could hear was Jake breathing behind me and the soft scuff of our shoes on the cave floor. The darkness and silence of the cave was as suffocating as I remembered, but there was nothing to do but move through it.

I had no idea how much time was passing—time seemed to work differently in the cave—but I was sure now that this was the right cave. The hairs on my arms were standing on end again, and an unnatural wind blew against my face from time to time. We were getting closer.

We reached a place where the tunnel turned right. I hurried around the corner, urgency overriding my caution—

I collided with a warm body in the darkness. My flashlight dropped from my hands, and I fumbled to pick it up, then finally managed to grab it and shine it challengingly at the person I'd crashed into.

I nearly dropped the light again. It was my mom.

Her face was dirty, a bruise standing out on her left cheekbone. At the sight of me, her eyes widened, and then she launched herself forward and wrapped her arms around me.

"Oh, Alisha, thank God," she whispered.

After systematically losing every adult in my life, I couldn't help clinging to my mother and resting my head in the warm, comfortable crook of her shoulder.

"Mom, what happened to you? How did you get here?"

"Lucas betrayed us," she said quietly. "They took him over, and he betrayed us."

I stared at her, my mouth gone dry. "No."

"I didn't want to believe it either, but it's true. They got your grandmother, but I managed to get away. I figured they would be trying to open the rift again, so I headed here. I know there isn't much I can do to stop them, but I couldn't just stand by. I had to do something." She stroked my hair with more tenderness than she'd shown me since I was a kid. "And I guess you did too."

I shook my head. "But Uncle Lucas— He couldn't have betrayed us. He couldn't have."

"Honey, if they took him over, then it wasn't him who did it."

"You don't understand," I said impatiently. "He *couldn't* get taken over."

Agitated, I pulled my phone out of my pocket. I'd meant to just pull up the text message and show it to Mom, show her it was clearly someone who was not Uncle Lucas texting me, but my fumbling fingers hit the letter *K* and Send.

Something buzzed in Mom's pocket.

I took a small step backward. "Is that— Is that Uncle Lucas's phone? Why do you have it?"

"He dropped it," Mom said. "I picked it up so he couldn't use it to contact you."

"Mrs. Howard."

Bella came forward from the shadows. The others had stayed quiet up until now, hidden around the corner of the tunnel, and I prayed they would stay there.

"Bella," Mom said, in what now seemed to me to be a brittle kind of voice. "You're here too? I'm glad you're all right."

"I just wanted to ask you," she said, "if my mom was okay."

Mom's face went blank, just for a second, as if she had no idea what Bella was talking about. Then it morphed into a reassuring smile. "Oh! Yes, she's fine."

I took another step back, putting me shoulder to shoulder with Bella. My thoughts tracked backward, and I remembered the night before, Grandma opening a hole in the barrier around the house so Uncle

Lucas's soul could get back to his body. I remembered both of us rushing over to the couch, neither of us looking at the hole as Grandma hastily closed it up.

What if something had come through it? What if something had followed Uncle Lucas and come through the barrier, come into the house?

Details filtered back to me. Mom had been unusually quiet at breakfast. She hadn't argued at all about having Martina's spirit go into her. And we only had Mom's word that Martina had reached her safely, that she was even still in there at all. Someone had betrayed us. Someone had told Officer Shelby where to find Bella and me.

Lucas betrayed us, she'd said.

I knew he hadn't. I knew it deep in my bones. And that meant only one thing.

Mom had.

I watched her face harden. Darkness came into her eyes, and she smiled.

"Well, it was worth a try," she said, and then she attacked.

She came at me with the grace and quickness of a panther, her fist swinging at my face, but I ducked and her knuckles slammed into the wall of the cave instead. She hissed in pain and lashed out with one long-nailed hand, but I was already moving away. Bella swept out her leg to try to trip her, but Not-Mom leaped lightly over it and jabbed Bella in the ribs with her elbow. Bella staggered back but recovered quickly, and there was a moment when the three of us stood panting in battle stances, staring at each other.

"You took her last night, didn't you?" I said.

Her face twisted into another awful smile. "She was asleep. She never even knew what was happening." She flexed her fingers. "But you will."

I tensed again, dread growing within me as I realized that even with Bella and I both giving it our all we might not win this fight.

A rush of wind gusted past us, picked up Not-Mom, and slammed her into the far wall of the cave. The impact knocked her head back against the stone, and she fell to the floor and lay still.

We spun around to find Aggie standing behind us, one hand extended and a look of anguished determination on her face.

"Are you okay?" she asked.

I somehow found the breath to answer. "Yes. God. Thank you."

She nodded but didn't look happy about it, and Jake and Gwen joined us, looking pale.

"First Dad, now Mom," Jake said. "And where are Uncle Lucas and Grandma?"

"I don't know." I'd been holding back the grief as best I could, but it was hard not to think about the fact that I had no idea where my mom's spirit was, and Grandma could have been taken, and because Uncle Lucas couldn't be taken, he might very well be dead, and Dad was somewhere in the depths of my mind but still wasn't answering, and what were the chances that any of us were going to survive this anyway?

It was all just a lot. My defenses wobbled, and I thought I might break down sobbing right here in the middle of the cave.

But that wouldn't help anyone, would it?

Later, I promised my grief. *Later, after all this is over.*

I took a shaky breath and drew myself up to my full height. "Come on. We must be getting close."

We were. A few minutes later, we were there.

Chapter Nineteen

No one was guarding the chamber, but they probably figured they didn't have to. The cave entrance was secure, and I doubted they were on high alert when, let's face it, they'd taken over pretty much everyone in town who could possibly be a threat to them.

Everyone except us.

I peered around the corner into the chamber. The candles had been relit, casting a weird, flickering glow around the chamber, and I could see shadowy, bodiless vesu soaring around the room, sticking close to the rocky ceiling but occasionally ducking down to dart past the candles or swirl around the figure that stood in the center of the room.

It was Mari, of course. She was still wearing her sweatshirt, jeans, and sneakers ensemble, and it was strange to see her gazing at the rift with such a cold, alien expression on her young face. The rift was a dark gash in the stone of the wall, barely wider than my hand, but as I watched, another of the vesu squeezed out of it and joined the mass swirling at the ceiling.

Martina and my dad were there too. They bowed to Mari as she strode to a ring of candles and lowered herself regally to sit within them. It was practically the same ritual Bella and I had stumbled onto the day before, except instead of a rift, it would become a gateway, and when night fell, enough vesu could pour out of this cave to take over the entire world.

Unless we stopped them.

I ducked back and motioned to the group. We backtracked down the tunnel and around a corner, just far enough to be out of sight and earshot. When the details of our battle plan were ironed out, we all spent a moment looking at one another with the knowledge that this could be the last time we did so.

And then, because time was short, we turned and headed to the chamber. As we walked, Bella took my hand and squeezed it. I squeezed hers back, wishing I had time to tell her how much she'd meant to me over this short time, but I also knew I didn't have to. She knew.

Just short of the chamber doorway, Aggie started chanting. It was quiet, so quiet I could barely hear it, and I knew Mari, Martina, and my dad definitely wouldn't be able to. A barrier sprang up around our group, and we fell into the formation we'd settled on: Bella and I in front, Jake and Gwen in back, Aggie and Grandma's spell book protected in the middle. Wreathed in blue light, we strode forward.

Mari didn't move when she saw us, except to lift an eyebrow and gesture vaguely at Martina and my dad. Both of them began chanting, while Mari closed her eyes and held her hand out to the rift. God, she was doing it now. She was opening it *now*.

I didn't need to glance at Bella—she felt the same urgency I did, and we both hurried forward, the others and the barrier moving with us.

The bodiless vesu swarmed around us, searching for cracks in our defenses, sizzling against the magic that protected us, and I wondered if we could just barge forward until the barrier itself knocked Mari back. But before we could test the theory, Martina snapped a hand toward Mari and a sphere of red light formed around her. When our barrier touched it, the two magics sizzled against each other and Aggie yelped as if she'd been burned.

Not-Dad was throwing bolts of energy at us, and now that Mari was protected, Martina had turned her attention to hurling streams of ice in our direction. The magics pinged harmlessly off our barrier, but a glance back at Aggie showed she was sweating. I couldn't help thinking about how long it had been since she'd done any real magic and wondered how long she could keep this up. And we hadn't even gotten to the tough part yet.

"Okay, Plan B!" I shouted.

We all jumped apart, Aggie's chanting rising furiously, and miraculously, it worked. The barrier broke into five pieces and we each found our bodies being hugged by blue light, individual magic armor that would hopefully keep the vesu away from us until we could get this done.

I headed for Martina and Dad while Bella ran for her sister. Jake and Gwen had taken up a protective position in front of Aggie, who sat on the floor to concentrate on her spell casting. She looked pale already, and I figured individual barriers like this had to take a lot more energy. I prayed she had enough.

I swung a fist at Martina and was pleased when it connected with her left cheek. She fell backward, and I managed to plant a kick to my dad's chest that sent him flying to join her.

Sorry, Dad, I thought.

Before they could get back up, I ran to join Bella and found her standing helplessly at the edge of the red sphere, staring in at her sister but unable to get to her.

"Aggie!" I shouted.

"I can't pull down her barrier!" Aggie shouted back. "All I can do is try to seal the rift before she opens it."

Bella swore, and I almost did the same. I remembered Dad talking about how powerful Mari was, and I couldn't help wondering how Aggie could possibly compete with her. If we couldn't get to Mari, then this was just going to be a magical tug-of-war back and forth between her and Aggie, opening and closing the rift until one of them ran out of steam. And much as I wanted to believe in my sister, I was pretty sure Mari was going to win that fight.

I heard a grunt from behind me—Not-Dad had run past us to attack Aggie or at least distract her from her spell casting. I was just tensing my muscles to spring at him when Gwen's fist slammed into his jaw and sent him skidding across the floor. I caught a glimpse of Jake's impressed face before my attention was drawn back to Mari.

Her chanting had grown louder, a cold wind whipping through the chamber, and the blackness of the rift pulsed like a living thing. The edges of the gap began to crumble and stretch, and I knew Mari was succeeding.

"Aggie!" I screamed again.

"I'm trying! I just—might—not—be strong enough!"

"Then I bet you could use some help," said a gruff voice behind us.

I spun around. It was Grandma and, a few steps behind her, Uncle Lucas. They were both surrounded by barriers of their own, and they looked like they'd been through a war, battered and bruised, but standing. If they'd fought their way through the vesu outside, then it was a miracle they looked as good as they did. I wanted to ask where they'd come from and what had happened to them and a thousand other things, but instead I turned my attention to Martina and Dad, who were crawling to their feet again.

"Go!" I shouted at Lucas and Grandma. "We'll hold these two off!"

Grandma and Lucas lowered themselves to the stone floor by Aggie. The three of them joined hands and I felt the mood of the room start to change, the power shifting from dark, inky black to something lighter and more pure. A glow like sunshine grew around the three of them, and the vesu above them hissed and flew away as if it had burned them.

"You will not stop this!" Mari screamed. "This is our future!" She leaped to her feet and held her hand out to the rift. I could feel her willing it to open, using every ounce of her power and desperation to pull it open...open...

She was stronger than Aggie, and she was probably stronger than Uncle Lucas and Grandma, but I doubted she was stronger than all three of them.

I threw another punch at Martina, which she dodged, and I'd just delivered a satisfying kick to her chest when Not-Dad grabbed my wrist and held it, and I felt his fingers vibrating against my barrier. It must have hurt him, but he kept pressing and pressing, and pretty soon I could see his fingers melting through the magic and getting closer and closer to my skin. I tried to wrench away but couldn't get his hand to budge, and I knew instinctively that if his fingers broke my barrier, the rest of it would fall too, and I would be defenseless. The vesu would take me before I could even draw breath to scream for Aggie.

Oh, no you don't! came Dad's voice from my head, and before I could wonder what he was going to do, a flicker of white light materialized in front of me and I realized, half horrified and half amazed, that Dad had flung his spirit out of my body and, as a result, out of the barrier that protected me. He hovered there for an instant, then dove forward and disappeared into his old body.

The fingers wrenching their way through my barrier released me, and I leapt back and hugged my wrist to my chest. I stared at my dad's face, scarcely daring to hope or breathe, and watched as it contorted in discomfort, then confusion, and then pain. His head tilted back, and he screamed, loud and long, and I resisted the urge to press my hands over my ears.

"GET...OUT!" Dad bellowed. A shadow erupted from his chest and was flung hard at the opposite wall of the cave.

Dad turned to me with joy and astonishment on his face, and I blinked back tears at the realization that it was him—it was really him. He'd gotten his body back, and he was here with us, ready to fight.

Dad's joy turned to determination, and he spoke a few words to bring a barrier up around his body.

"Much better," he said, and I'd never been so glad to hear his voice before in my life. "Now let's finish this." He joined Uncle Lucas, Aggie, and Grandma, and it was then I realized Grandma was no longer holding hands with the others. She had gotten to her feet and was standing with her eyes closed, chanting something different from the others.

"We summon you," she said in deep, resonant tones. At the sound of her voice, the vesu swirling above us all shivered, as if something had grabbed them for an instant and then let go. "Brothers and sisters of the darkness, creatures who call themselves the vesu, creatures who are trespassing in our world, we summon you. We summon you to this place. We summon you."

"No!" Mari screamed, but it was too late.

Grandma lifted her arms over her head, and when she opened her eyes, they glowed like two blazing suns.

"WE SUMMON YOU!" she roared, and a portal snapped open in front of her like a black hole. At first, I thought it was there to suck in the vesu already in the room, but instead, shadowy creatures poured out of it by the dozens, by the hundreds. A wind swept through the room and caught them in its grips as they left the portal, forming a great, terrible cyclone of screeching shadows.

I still didn't quite understand what was happening, until a shadow was sucked from Martina's chest, at which point the protective red sphere around Mari quivered and finally vanished. Mari's eyes were wide and horrified as another shadow was drawn out of her body, and both her shadow and Martina's went flailing up into the cyclone. Martina and Mari dropped lifelessly to the ground, and I realized Grandma was using the summoning spell, the one she'd used to call Gwen's spirit back to her body, to summon *all* the vesu, all the ones that had come into our world.

At last, when there were no more vesu to come through the portal, Grandma snapped it closed with a flick of her wrist. Using both hands, she made a sweeping motion as if pushing the cyclone of vesu toward the dimensional rift, and it went. The vesu were pushed nearer and nearer to the doorway back to their own terrible dimension, and I could feel their panic, their terror, and their desperation. For the first time I wished there was some way we could help them without losing ourselves in the process.

"Wait!" Bella screamed.

Grandma hesitated, and before I could ask Bella what she was thinking, she ran to the rift and pressed her hands against it. "Mari! If you're in there, if you can hear me, this is your last chance! You have to come back! Please, if you can hear me, come back! It's me! It's Bella! Come back to me!"

"I can't hold them much longer!" Grandma grunted, and Bella gave her an anguished look but moved back from the rift.

Grandma made one last great pushing motion with her hands, and the cyclone surged forward to the rift and disappeared inside. She dropped to her knees on the cave floor. "Now!" she gasped.

Aggie, Dad, and Uncle Lucas raised their hands as one toward the rift and all chanted the same words, over and over, their eyes squeezed shut and their faces taut with concentration. I held my breath, hoping, praying, pleading. This had to work. This *had* to work! The rift shuddered and seemed to be closing, the stone mending back together, the dark glimpse of the vesu's world fading. There was one final grinding of stone, a strange flicker of white light—

All the candles in the room went out at once, and everything was still.

I stood in the darkness breathing fast, hardly daring to wonder what had happened, if we'd done it, if we'd succeeded.

A match was lit, illuminating Uncle Lucas's tired, bruised face from below. He moved over to the cave wall where the rift had been, and I saw the wall was smooth again. Even the charred mark that had been there before was gone.

I sank to the ground and dropped my head into my hands, not sure if I wanted to laugh or cry.

The dimensional rift was sealed. The vesu were gone.

We'd done it.

"Mari?" came a whisper through the silence.

I lifted my head. Bella's face was illuminated by soft white light, light that emanated from a tiny, flickering spirit floating in the air in front of her. The light bobbed up and down as if in answer to her question, and tears shone in Bella's eyes as she held out her hands and let the spirit rest in her palms. Mari's spirit? But something was wrong with it. It was so small, the light so low, and it flickered like a candle about to go out.

"She's dying," Uncle Lucas said, very softly. "Human spirits aren't meant to exist in the vesu realm, and I can only imagine what being there for all those years has done to her. Death isn't possible in the vesu realm, but now that she's back in our world..."

"No," Bella choked. She held her cupped hands close to her tear-streaked face. "No, please. I finally got you back..."

The light flickered again, then with what seemed like a great effort, it fluttered up to Bella's forehead and rested against her skin. Bella sat up suddenly straight, her eyes going wide, and then she closed her eyes and nodded. "I understand," she whispered.

The light floated back to Bella's hands, flickered once more, and disappeared.

Bella stared at her empty palms for a long moment before she dropped them down into her lap. "She said, 'Thank you,' and 'I'm sorry.'"

We all sat in a stunned, mourning silence. Someone lit the candles, illuminating the room more fully, and my eyes settled on Martina. She lay limply on the cave floor, and I couldn't bear to think that Bella, who had just lost her sister, might now be about to lose her mother too. I tried not to think of my own mother, who was probably still lying on the cave floor not far away from here.

"What happens to them?" I asked. "What happens to all the people who got taken?"

Grandma still knelt on the floor, looking exhausted. "Wait until nightfall. If their spirits are still out there, they'll feel drawn to their bodies now that they're empty. They'll find them."

"*If* their spirits are still out there?"

"There's a lot we don't know about things like this. And there's a lot that can happen to a spirit that's torn out of its body. I hope all of them had sense enough to hide away somewhere safe, and that now that their bodies are waiting for them, they'll find them, and things can go back to the way they were. But some of them might not come back. They could've gone out into the sunlight, not knowing, or the vesu could've destroyed them. There's just no way to know."

I met Bella's eyes and tried to send all the love and support I could in her direction. The sadness didn't leave her expression, but she gave me a soft, grateful smile, and I vowed that whatever happened, I would be there to make sure she got through it all right.

Chapter Twenty

The funeral was held on a rainy day in early October, and I held my umbrella in one hand and Bella's hand in the other. The grass of the cemetery was too soft under our feet, shifting with every step, but we were still able to make our careful way to the grave and the coffin suspended over it.

My family was already seated under the awning that had been erected to keep out the rain. They were in one of the back rows of folding chairs, Mom and Dad sitting next to each other looking somber and holding hands, Aggie, Jake, Gwen, Grandma, and Uncle Lucas beside them. I figured Bella would want to sit in the front row, but instead she led me to the same row my family sat in, and we ended up taking the two empty chairs next to Uncle Lucas. I didn't comment because I understood. This was my family, but it was hers now too.

The rain pattered softly on the awning over our heads, and after a time, the minister stepped up to the podium.

"We are gathered today," she said, "to say goodbye to someone who has been taken from us far too soon. Someone deeply loved, who will of course also be deeply missed. I'd like to ask the person who knew her best to speak to you now."

At first, I was afraid the minister was going to call on Bella to speak and knew she would hate that, but instead the woman gestured, and Martina Rodriguez stepped up to the podium. Her red hair was damp from the rain, and she looked understandably weary, but there was still an undeniable feeling of strength to her as she gazed out at the assembled faces.

"We are here today," she said, "to say goodbye to my daughter Mari."

She told us stories about Mari as a child and young woman, and I got to know a good, sweet, inquisitive person who had loved reading books and writing poems and learning new things, someone who had been compassionate enough to try to help when she heard a cry from across the dimensional wall. I wished I could've known her. I had the feeling I would've liked her a lot.

Martina didn't mention what had really happened to Mari, of course, and the official story was that her body had been found in the cave after all these years, that she'd been the victim of a cave-in and had died there because no one had heard her screams for help. It was a believable enough lie, which our operatives in the medical examiner's office were sure to back up, and it had the added bonus of giving the city a good reason to board up the entrance to the cave to prevent anyone else from stumbling into it. The Guardians would still be keeping an eye on it, but at least there was much less chance of anyone else wandering in there, whether summoned by vesu or not.

Of course, this wasn't much comfort when we were burying a girl who should've had a long life ahead of her, but at least it was something.

The night the rift was sealed, Bella had told me more about Mari. We'd lain together in the darkness of her room with our arms wrapped around each other, clinging to the reality of both of us being alive, safe, and together. In the dark safety of the night, Bella had whispered her story to me.

"Mari was the only real friend I had," she said. "Mom never had time for us, and I didn't get along with the kids at school, so Mari was my everything. As we got older, though, we drifted apart, especially when I turned thirteen and started really focusing on training to join the Guardians. I got so wrapped up in Guardian stuff that I stopped spending so much time with Mari, and maybe if I hadn't... I don't know.

"But even though I was busy, I still noticed when something changed. Mari was always kind of secretive—she didn't like me reading her stories or her poems or looking at her drawings—but this was different. She was distracted all the time, and I started hearing her leaving her room at night and not coming back for hours. Too bad Mom wasn't head of the council back then, or someone definitely would've seen her going and stopped her, but no one was watching, so no one saw. No one but me. Finally, one night, I followed her, and that's when I found her at the cave.

"She was sitting on the floor in that chamber, alone, and she was talking to someone. I heard her say something about being ready, and she sounded really happy about it. Then there was a pause like she was listening to someone, and she said, 'Do you think it'll be dangerous?' I got this feeling, like all the hairs rising on my arms, and even though I couldn't hear anything with my ears, for a second it was like I was hearing a voice in my mind. I couldn't make out what it was saying, but it was there, and I got freaked out and ran. I guess I was still pretty shaken up when I got home, because I accidentally set off the security system and woke up my mom.

"I didn't want to tell on Mari, but Mom checked her room and saw she was gone. And I guess I really did feel like there was something wrong about what Mari was doing because I told my mom about the cave. She actually looked scared. She made me promise to stay in the house, and she left right away, and I guess she must've called your dad and had him meet her at the cave. That was the night Mari disappeared.

"The next day, Mom told me Mari was missing. She said she'd gone to the cave but Mari hadn't been there, and I believed her because she looked so upset. I didn't realize she was upset because Mari *had* been there, and Mom had to watch her get possessed by a vesu and get her soul sucked into another dimension. I wish I could get angry at her for not telling me, but what good would it have done if she had? None.

"But it just doesn't seem fair. Mari was a good person. She was so good that she wanted to help a bunch of body-stealing shadows, and what did she get for it? Five years of torture in a dark dimension and then death."

Bella's voice cracked and I held her more tightly.

"You know what she told me, Howard? When her spirit touched me, it was like she was a part of me for a second, and it all flashed through my head. Floating in that dark place, suffering, and feeling like she was dying but not able to die... But she still managed to make *friends*. Can you believe that? That was how she stayed sane. She floated around and when she ran into a vesu's spirit, she joined with it and talked to it and shared her story with it. She went around telling all these vesu about Earth and her life, and you know what? It actually seemed to help them. It gave them *hope*. My sister got her soul sucked out of her body and spent five years trapped in what was essentially hell, and she used that time to make other people's lives better.

"I told you in the cave that she said 'Thank you' and 'Sorry,' but she also said, 'Forgive them.' It was the last thing she told me. And it's the one thing I don't want to do, but for her sake I guess I have to try."

Luckily, or maybe miraculously, Mari seemed to be the only one who had truly been lost to the vesu. One by one, wandering souls found their way back to their bodies, called there as if by some innate homing signal, and life in town was gradually getting back to normal. There had been no news reports about the weirdness that had happened. I figured everyone had collectively decided it was all too unbelievable and must have been some mass hallucination because what was the alternative? That they had all been booted out of their bodies and spent a day floating around in the ether? That shadow creatures from another dimension had tried to end life as we knew it on Earth?

It was all too unthinkable, so most people shuddered, shrugged, and got down to the business of forgetting it had ever happened. It was a coping mechanism, I figured, and I half wished I had the luxury of forgetting about it myself.

But, I thought, glancing down at Bella's warm hand wrapped in mine, *there are some things I'm very glad not to forget about.*

After Martina finished her eulogy for Mari, she looked in Bella's direction as if for permission, and I guess she found it because she came and sat in the empty seat next to her. When Martina rested her hand lightly on Bella's arm, the expression on Bella's face was not one of irritation or anger, but of warmth.

When the minister finished, Bella and Martina got to their feet and headed to the coffin to say their goodbyes, and I hung back to let them have that moment to themselves. Beside me, Uncle Lucas smiled and patted my hand, and I looked down across the row at the warm faces of my family and my best friend.

    We'd done it. We'd come through this, and we were still whole, still a unit, still together.

    We were still a family.

Chapter Twenty-One

After the funeral services ended, we all headed to Grandma's house for a late lunch and some much-needed rest. Martina was invited too, and I was pleased to see her and Mom talking civilly as they filled their plates from the buffet Grandma had set up. I doubted they would ever be close, but if they could be in the same room without wanting to kill each other? Fantastic. Especially since I had a feeling our families were going to be spending a lot more time together from now on.

Mom was also a lot nicer to Uncle Lucas, and I'd finally figured out that she'd mistrusted him for all these years because she'd known about his less-than-human origins. After everything that happened, it seemed like he'd proven himself to her, or maybe she was just more in the mood to be forgiving after all we'd been through. Either way, it was nice to see.

Uncle Lucas had finally told us what happened that day after they left Grandma's house for Guardians HQ. Apparently the vesu inside Mom had waited until they were driving through a deserted stretch of woods, and then she had wrenched the wheel out of Uncle Lucas's hands and steered them all off the road, down a hillside, and into a tree. The car had been totaled, making it impossible for them to get to headquarters as they'd planned, and Grandma and Uncle Lucas had been knocked out, whether by the crash or by Not-Mom, it was impossible to say. When they came to, Mom was gone, and they'd put things together and come to the cave after Bella and me. Thank goodness they had too. If they hadn't, I doubted any of us would be here today to enjoy the buffet.

I looked around the room at my family and thought again about how lucky I was to have them and how lucky we all were to have come out of this all right. I'd always figured that being a hero meant being brave enough to do things on your own, but every single person in this house had done something to help save the world, and none of us could have done it alone.

My eyes settled on Mom, standing by herself in the corner of the room, poking at her potato salad with her fork.

Even though we'd all come out of this thing more or less okay, I really had almost lost both my parents—and everyone else, to be honest—and it had made me realize that while Dad and I were still and had always been pretty close, Mom and I had definitely drifted apart. Martina had told Mom to leave the Guardians to spend more time with her kids, but Mom hadn't been doing that, had she? She'd been shutting herself up in her studio or just generally keeping herself closed off from all of us, and I wanted to know why.

I waited until we were alone in Grandma's kitchen, doing the dishes while everyone else worked off lunch by taking a walk in the post-rain sunshine.

"Mom, why did you really leave the Guardians?"

Mom's hands froze in the act of scrubbing a greasy pan. "Why are you asking that now?"

"I know Martina said you ought to leave, but she wasn't even head of the council back then. And even if she had been, you didn't have to listen to her. It was still your decision."

Mom was silent for so long I wondered if she was going to answer me at all.

"I just want to know more about you," I said, almost pleading. "I want to understand."

Her expression softened, and she sighed and turned to lean her back on the edge of the counter. "Martina did suggest I leave the Guardians," Mom said in a quiet, measured voice. "It was right around the time Mari disappeared, so I knew why she was doing it. It wasn't her place at all, but I understood. That's not why I ended up retiring."

"Why did you, then? Did something happen?"

"A few months after Mari's disappearance, there was an altercation with some unfriendly NEBs who didn't want to leave Earth. My counterpart was out of town, so I decided to take them on alone. I was the famous Helen Howard, the one who got called in for all the most dangerous assignments, and I figured I could handle it. Turns out I couldn't." She lifted the fabric of her silky green shirt, and I was stunned to see a long, puckered scar slicing diagonally across her stomach. "It almost killed me. If backup hadn't gotten there in time, it probably would have."

She pulled her shirt back down, but the image of the scar was burned forever into my mind.

"How did we not know about this?"

"I didn't want you to know, so I got your dad to tell you Aunt Celia needed me in California to help with her move. All that time, I was in the Guardians hospital in Baltimore recovering."

My mind flashed back to the time in question, and I remembered Mom coming home three weeks later looking tired and washed out. I figured she'd just been working too hard or Aunt Celia had been driving her crazy like usual, but *this* was what had really happened? She'd been lying in a hospital bed for all that time healing from a wound that had almost killed her?

"Mom, I get why you didn't want to tell us, but I, for one, would've liked to know. We would've come to visit you; we would've spent time with you. You didn't have to do it all alone."

"I felt like I did," Mom said. "Maybe that was a mistake. But after that, your father and I got to talking about how it would've affected you kids if I hadn't made it, and I decided it was time for me to retire. So I did."

Ordinarily I wouldn't have pushed for more information, but I knew that now was a time when I had to.

"Did you ever regret it?"

A pained look touched Mom's features. "Every day. In the Guardians, I had purpose. I knew who I was and what I was doing with my life. But outside? I was nothing. Nothing I did seemed to matter to anyone anymore, and it was hard. It still is."

I studied her in the warm glow from the kitchen window, and it seemed insane to me that I'd never thought to wonder how she felt about all this. She'd been a Guardian for most of my childhood, and I'd seen how she loved it, how she came home energized and headed for her studio with a spring in her step. And I'd seen it all change when she retired, but I'd been too wrapped up in my own life to even spare a thought to hers.

"Why don't you join back up?"

Mom gave a sharp laugh. "Right."

"No, I mean it. If being a Guardian is what you want to do, what feels right to you, then you should do it. And yeah, it's dangerous. But it's also important. And if Aggie, Jake, and I are what's stopping you from being one, then this is me officially telling you, from your children, that we don't want you to do that. We want you to be happy, and you're clearly not happy now. You haven't been for a really long time, and we— *I* never noticed."

"I didn't want you to notice," Mom said.

She stood with her arms folded, a thoughtful look on her face. Finally, she gave a tight smile. "I have to say, it felt good getting into my old battle gear again. Maybe I'll talk to Martina. I don't think I want to return to full Guardian status, but maybe I could do some part-time work, or work on the training side of things or something."

I grinned and put my arm around her, and to my surprise, she turned it into a full-on hug. She didn't say anything, but she didn't have to. I pulled back from her, feeling like we'd taken one important step closer to each other, and if I had anything to say about it, it wouldn't be the last.

After we'd finished the dishes, Mom headed outside to catch up with the others, but I stayed behind. I'd seen Grandma slip past us and head upstairs about fifteen minutes earlier, and she hadn't come back down yet. Drying my hands as best I could on an already sodden dish towel, I followed the slight creaking I could hear overhead up to the big bedroom on the second floor.

Grandma stood facing the bureau, and on top of it was a wooden box with a padlock that glowed faintly red. She was holding her palm over the box, her eyes closed and a crease of concentration in her brow.

"Is it still in there?" I asked.

Grandma didn't seem surprised to hear my voice. "I can't tell. I'm not sure if my summoning spell was strong enough to get past the enchantments on the box and pull that vesu out of there along with all the others. And if it wasn't, then any vesu that was being contained like this is still here in our world."

"Uncle Lucas is still here too," I said. This had been bothering me for a while, but I hadn't been able to find a good time to bring it up. "Did you know, when you cast that spell that it wouldn't get him too?"

"Not sure what you mean," Grandma said, but I was pretty sure she did.

"I mean, you summoned all the vesu in our world. That could've applied to Uncle Lucas. We could've lost him because of that spell."

Grandma's jaw tightened. Her voice was soft when she answered. "Sweetie, I had to take that chance. The last thing I wanted was to lose my own son, but if it meant saving everybody else, saving the world? I had to do it."

I understood. I really did. "Why do you think it didn't take him?"

She gave a tight smile. "Because I summoned the vesu, and he's not a vesu, not anymore. He's as human as you or I, maybe not by birth, but definitely by the life he's lived. And the life he's going to keep living, thank goodness. I just hope he'll be more careful from now on. I hope you'll all be more careful."

"You know, I'm not going to quit the Guardians," I said in a rush. "It's who I am, and I can't change that no matter how much I want you to be in my life."

Grandma's expression softened. "I know, sweetheart. I guess I can live with that. It hasn't been easy, living without all of you for all these years. I thought I was doing what was right, that it would change your parents' minds or at least make it so I didn't have to go through the pain of losing you if the worst happened, but it wouldn't have helped. If we'd lost you, it would've hurt just as much if I was out of your life as if I'd been in it. Probably more. And as it is, it looks like you're one hell of a Guardian and turning into one hell of a woman too."

I blinked a sudden mistiness from my eyes and grabbed Grandma in a tight hug. It was turning into one heck of a hugging day. We clung to each other for a moment, then released each other and stepped back.

Our gazes turned, as one, to the box.

"What are you going to do with it?" I asked.

"Keep an eye on it," she said. "It should be safe up in the attic for now."

"You wouldn't rather give it to the Guardians?"

Grandma gave a humorless laugh, and I knew I shouldn't even have asked.

"It'll be fine here," she said. "Probably a lot safer too. The enchantment on it's not going to wear off for a very long time."

"And when it does?"

She smiled faintly. "Well, let's just hope your little team manages to get the vesu sorted out by then."

The team had been Aggie's idea. She'd already fully adopted Bella as her second sister, and the three of us had spent some time talking about Mari, what had happened to her, and the vesu in general. After hearing what Mari had gone through in the vesu dimension, Aggie had been adamant that the vesu clearly weren't innately bad, they were just trapped in a bad place and trying to find a way out of it. Desperation and pain fueled them, not malice.

We'd approached Martina about it, and I'd seen her sharp features soften as we explained our idea, and where it had come from.

"Mari wanted to help them," Aggie said with her own particular brand of gentle firmness. "And I think we owe it to her memory to try to do what we can for them."

Martina's voice was low and cautious. "What do you suggest we do?"

"Up until now, the vesu have been reaching out through the dimensions, trying to make contact with someone. But what if we try to contact them? We can find out more about them and their world, and if there's no way to make their world better, then maybe we can move them. There are so many dimensions out there, and there must be one they can exist in safely and with no danger to anyone else. My suggestion," Aggie said, drawing herself up to her full height, "is that we put together a team of researchers and spell casters who can work together to contact the vesu, assess their situation, and locate a dimension we can relocate them to. It might not be possible, but we'll never know until we try."

Much to my surprise, Martina had easily agreed, and the team had been assembled almost immediately. There'd been some naysayers on the council—Gideon in particular, who was still pretty annoyed that Martina had been reinstated despite all that had happened—but even they had had to admit that if Aggie's plan worked, it would provide a better and more long-lasting protection from the vesu than anything else possibly could.

And when I thought about Uncle Lucas, hands down one of the best people I'd ever known, and how he had come from that same dark place and had managed to turn into such an amazing human being, I knew we owed it to the vesu to try to give them that same chance. And we owed it to Mari too. She'd given her life trying to help them, and maybe it would give her some peace, wherever she was, to know we were trying to help them too.

*

Later that afternoon, Bella and I sat together on the swing on Grandma's back porch. The fields were golden again, this time with the light of the afternoon sun as it dipped lower in the sky. Evening was coming, and night after that, but we didn't need to be afraid of it anymore.

We sat quietly swinging for what felt like a long time, our fingers intertwined and our shoulders pressed warmly together.

"How are you doing?" I asked after a while.

Bella didn't answer at first, and I got the impression she was really considering the question.

"I think I'm okay." Her voice was soft, and there was a new level of peace to it that I'd never heard there before. "My sister's gone, and I don't think I'll ever stop missing her. But after all these years, I never thought I'd get to see her or talk to her again, and I got to do both. I got to say goodbye. It seems like such a little thing, but it meant so much. And my mom... It's the first time we've really talked in years, and I feel like we might actually find some way to like each other again. It's weird, but I think— I think I'm more okay than I've been in a really long time."

"And all it took was one little invasion," I said.

Bella laughed and leaned her head against my shoulder. I looked down at our intertwined fingers and felt a surge of pure, unabashed happiness.

"Hey, Howard?" Bella said.

"Hm?"

"If none of this had happened, do you think we ever would've figured it out?"

I thought I knew what she meant, but I wanted to be sure. "Figured what out?"

"This," she said, nodding to our clasped hands. "Us. That maybe we didn't hate each other after all."

"I don't know. But it did happen, and we did figure it out, so I guess it doesn't matter."

I could hear the smile in Bella's voice. "I think we would've figured it out eventually. Maybe not this soon, but eventually? Definitely."

"How can you be so sure?" It seemed important.

She lifted her head to gaze into my eyes. "I just am. What, are you waiting for me to say something sappy like 'Love finds a way' or 'I can't imagine a world where I didn't fall for you'? Well, I'm not going to, so don't hold your breath."

I grinned at her, though the words had knocked the breath from my lungs. "You kind of already did."

Her eyes widened; then she sighed and rolled her eyes at me. "Just shut up and kiss me," she said, so I did.

About the Author

T.J. Baer is a queer trans author of novels and short fiction. Born in Western Pennsylvania, he currently resides in his adopted hometown of Chicago with two cats and a well-stocked cupboard of tea. When not writing, T.J. can be found either discussing queer media on his YouTube channel or failing to escape from murderous ghosts on Twitch.

Email
tjbaerwrites@gmail.com

Facebook
www.facebook.com/tjbaerofficial

Twitter
@TJBaerAuthor

Website
www.tjbaer.com

YouTube
www.youtube.com/c/thomistrans

Twitch
www.twitch.tv/thom_is_trans

www.ninestarpress.com

www.facebook.com/ninestarpress

www.facebook.com/groups/NineStarNiche

www.twitter.com/ninestarpress

www.instagram.com/ninestarpress

Made in the USA
Columbia, SC
25 April 2024